MIC DROP

A HIGH-RISE MYSTERY

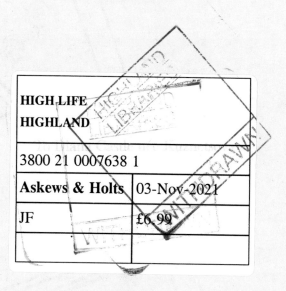
SHARNA JACKSON

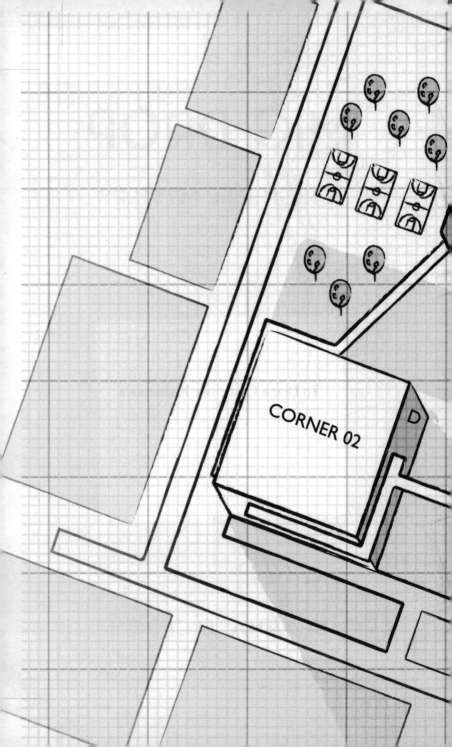

MIC DROP

A HIGH-RISE MYSTERY

SHARNA JACKSON

Published by Knights Of
Knights Of Ltd, Registered Offices:
Kalculus, 119 Marylebone Road, London, NW1 5PU

www.knightsof.media
First published 2020
002

Written by Sharna Jackson
Text © Sharna Jackson, 2020
Cover art by Wumzum [Wumi Olaosebikan], 2020
Map illustration © Paul Coulbois (Astound US Inc.)
All rights reserved
The moral right of the author and illustrator has been asserted

Set in Baskerville Regular / 12 pt
Design and Typeset by Marssaié Jordan
Printed and bound in the UK

A CIP catalogue record for this book will be available from the British Library

ISBN: PB: 9781913311032

2 4 6 8 10 9 7 5 3

CORNER 01

A B C

THE REC

F E

CORNER 03

• Site Office
A HKW Centre
B Better Buy
C Bermuda's Public
  House
D Clarke's Flat
E The Green Room
F The Roof

EXCLUSIVE: TrojKat Signs To Arcadia

Melinda Tuza, Senior Reporter

August 11, 14:15

After intense speculation, RME can exclusively report that TrojKat, South London's streaming sensation, has signed on the dotted line with New York-based record label Arcadia in a seven-figure deal.

The previously-unsigned TrojKat (known to friends and family as Katarzyna Clarke) has committed to a five-album deal at the age of 23. Her new label-mates at Arcadia include the chart-topping Dame GoGo, AKA Swigs, Kay-V and Lunero.

The Cusp singer said: 'I'm delighted. I'm amazed. I've mostly worked alone… tirelessly… my entire life to make my music, so I'm thrilled to be working with the dedicated, supportive team at Arcadia to bring my vision to the whole world.'

'TrojKat has a rare freshness and an exciting energy,' remarked Jessica Holbrook, Director of Artist Development at Arcadia. 'Her talent for lyrics is especially exceptional. We're so ready to take her – and her genius – to the next level. Welcome to the Arcadia family, TrojKat!'

But local fans shouldn't worry: TrojKat's transatlantic deal does not mean she'll be leaving the UK any time soon. 'I love London, and I have something very special planned for the video of Cusp. Watch this space!'

They didn't listen to me.

If they had, perhaps this wouldn't be happening.

Perhaps she wouldn't be looking me in the eye, her face twisted with terror, as she succumbed to the inevitable.

I will never forget that face. Never.

Katarzyna 'Kat' Clarke. 23. Better known as TrojKat.

Her talent was undoubtedly on the rise, but her body was mere milliseconds away from a fatal fall.

This former resident of The Tri was definitely about to die.

Katarzyna fell.

I stood still, frozen on the spot. My heart raced in my chest. 500 beats per minute. I didn't lean to look over the side. Why would I? Zero desire. There were exactly 0.0 recurring reasons to witness her body meet the concrete. For what reason?

No, her expression was enough trauma. Enough trauma for an entire lifetime. Somewhere, in another dimension, possibly, Future Me was thanking Current Me for this wise decision.

Why were we here at all? How did all the small decisions we made through our lives lead us here tonight? Standing on the edge of a tower block, with Katarzyna's film crew – her four friends and colleagues – witnessing a pop star lose her life? My sister and fellow investigator Norva had said. 'Nik, you defo have to be involved, it's going to be awesome.'

It was 'awesome' in all the negative ways 'awesome' could be.

Wait, let me give you the facts.

The Tri – better known as The Triangle, consisting of three tall towers called Corners – is the estate where we live. We being Norva and I, and her best friend George.

Tonight, we found ourselves on the roof of Corner Three. Many meters in the sky, overlooking the entire city, participating in a video shoot for Katarzyna's new song, Cusp.

The song that was supposed to break her into the big leagues.

Katarzyna's scream curdled my blood, twisted my stomach,

implanted itself in my brain, never to leave. It was followed by a smacking, echoing thud I would never forget.

The worst sound I've ever heard.

It was the rope that broke this evening. Along with thousands of hearts – and Katarzyna's body.

TrojKat was dead. 31/10. 19:56.

A terrible, terrible accident.

Or so it seemed.

That's what everyone else said.

But not us.

I

Friday, 30 October. 18:02.

The sun had set. Two hours and one minute ago.

Pap's office. His desk lamp was on.

Pap. Joseph Alexander. 39. Our dad. Cool head. Kind heart. The Building Manager here on The Tri was working.

Or trying to.

He placed his thumbs on his temple and fashioned a sort of visor on his forehead with his fingers.

He tried to concentrate on his screen, but it was futile.

I sat at the other side of his desk. My feet swung gently against his leg.

I was content, mostly. 75% relaxed.

I typed a list of my top five favourite equations on my phone. Pi was winning, of course. How could it not?

'We're living at the cusp!'

A voice behind me.

That voice. The source of my 25% of discontent.

Norva Alexander. 13. Cascading braids, drama in spades. Sleuthing was her trade – or at least she wanted it to be when she was older. She stood in the corner of the office. She wasn't still, though. If only.

My sister is never still, unless something is seriously wrong.

Her phone in her left hand, a full can of Hola-Cola in her right. Black headphones (broken, but hastily fixed with yellowing sellotape) barely covered her ears.

Tinny music spilled into the room. She flipped her braids from her left shoulder, and over to her right.

She danced around her backpack. No, that's too generous – she stumbled with enthusiasm. Between breaths, she sang. No – again, too generous. She screeched in search of a key.

I didn't recognise the lyrics:

We're living at the cusp
Existing by the brink
What happens if we swim?
Do I sink?

Terrible. 4/10 – and that was generous.
I could feel Norva behind me.

From the corner of my left eye, I saw her hand approach my face. Her third attempt in the last fifteen minutes.

'Don't!' I warned. I rolled away from the desk and blocked her arm. 'Stop touching me! Respect my boundaries. I mean it.'

'But so much growth for three months, though' she shouted over her music.

'107 days,' I muttered.

'What'd you say? Eh – doesn't matter, I love it, truly.'

Norva took off her headphones. Thin music emanated from her neck. 'That barnet is serving me both body and movement. Imagine if you put some actual effort into a costume for tomorrow, Nik? You'd smash it.' She put her can to her lips and gulped.

'I'm not dressing up tomorrow. Or ever. I'm telling you now, like I've told you before, I don't believe in Halloween. It's unnecessary.'

'Yeah, so you say, but just listen, right. Hear me out, now. If we –'

I kicked Pap under the desk. 'Pap! tell her.'

'Norva please –' Pap said, not looking away from his screen '– and move your feet, Nik.'

'Alright, alright, I'll leave it,' said Norva. She raised her hands in the air, pretending to surrender. 'I get it, I hear you.'

She placed her palms on Pap's desk. 'I'm. Just. Buzzing. About. Tomorrow,' she said, slapping it between each word. The lamp shook. 'I cannot wait.'

'And I can't wait for you two to go back to school,' Pap muttered under his breath.

I detected a slight smile on his lips.

Norva kissed her teeth. 'Pap come on… cut me some slack! It's Halloween in a few hours. The reigning Queen of The Tri, excluding me, obvs, is coming home. Isn't that epic?!'

She crouched down and whispered in my ear. 'What an excellent addition to The Tri Files.' She stood up, slapping me on the back, before winking and taking another swig from her can.

The Tri Files. Our observations of occurrences on our estate. As Norva always says: 'If something's going down on The Tri, we know what's up.'

I looked up at her and rolled my eyes, but she had a point.

'It's only little Kat,' said Pap. 'Calm down.'

'Yeah, only TrojKat,' Norva replied. 'Only one of London's best new pop artists. Just a tiny one point eight million followers on Instagram, Pap. Only just signed a record deal that's going to change her life. Only –'

'Only me,' said a cool voice behind us.

2

'Oh my god,' whispered Norva, without turning around. 'She's here, isn't she?'

'She can hear you,' laughed Pap.

I spun in my chair. TrojKat stood in the doorway.

A tiny thin body, like a doll. Curly black hair, to her waist. Deep purple matte lipstick. Light brown skin, the whitest teeth.

She wore large sunglasses that covered at least a third of her small face, even though it was dark.

I scrunched my nose. How utterly pretentious, I thought.

I immediately told myself off for being so quick to judge her. Wait, Nik. Maybe she's nice. Don't be prejudiced!

Pap stood up. 'Kat,' he said with a chuckle. 'Welcome home, good to see you!' He opened his arms to embrace her.

She remained in the doorway. 'I bet it is,' she said through pursed lips. 'It's Katarzyna, now, OK?'

Noted. Katarzyna it was.

I glanced at Pap. He looked back at me with narrowed eyes.

My first impression was clearly the correct one.

Katarzyna removed her unnecessary glasses with a sigh. Deep brown eyes. Long spidery black lashes.

'How are you, Joe?' she said. She stepped into the office and looked around, frowning slightly. She ran a finger lightly across his desk. 'You're still… here?' She raised an eyebrow.

Pap cleared his throat. 'Yep, fourteen years and counting.' With his hands in his pockets, he briefly stood on his toes, and quickly put his heels back on the ground. 'They can't get rid of me!' he said with a laugh.

Katarzyna looked at her finger. She wiped it gingerly on her expensive-looking black leather trousers. 'Clearly.'

She looked at me. 'Which one are you?'

This woman was so rude.

'I'm Nik,' I said. I looked up and smiled, despite myself. I extended my hand, even though I really didn't want to. 'Nice to meet you. I've heard your music is popular. Congratulations.'

'Oh my god,' whispered Norva under her breath. 'So embarrassing.'

Katarzyna looked down at my hand. I was glad when

she didn't take it. 'It *is* popular. Thank you.'

She looked me up and down. I crossed my fingers in my lap. She cocked her head to the left. I turned away in my chair. 'You've grown,' she said. 'Congratulations.'

Norva laughed behind me.

She stood up straight and tall in front Katarzyna. She took a deep breath and grabbed her hand.

'Do you remember me? I'm Norva. I'm a big fan. Huge. Your songs are just beyond. I'm obsessed with *Cusp*. Obsessed. I was literally just listening to it! Clearly your best yet. Don't you think? Is that why Arcadia signed you? Got to be! It's a bop that speaks to me on levels you don't even know – it's exactly how I feel! You can't even imagine!' Norva jumped on the spot. 'When I found out you were coming home to film the video here, I died. Trust me, I died. Didn't I, Nik?'

'Well, no, you didn't – you're clearly alive.'

Norva shot me a look, and gripped Katarzyna's hand tighter. 'Anyway, yeah, sorry. I'm sorry, you're just a real inspiration to me. You're positive, you stay unbothered and keep it un-messy. I stan. Goals, you're goals. Also, you smell amazing. Just saying.'

While there was zero evidence of this positive attitude Norva spoke of, I could confirm the part about her scent.

Vanilla. Plums. Peonies. Hygiene was clearly a priority.

11

Katarzyna snatched her hand away. She reached into her bag and pulled out a small clear bottle. I peered at the label. Hand sanitiser. 'Appreciate the words – but don't touch people without their permission, yeah? I don't know where you've been.' She shuddered.

'Told you about the touching,' I said under my breath.

Norva looked at me and smiled sarcastically.

'I haven't forgotten what you did, you know?' Katarzyna said, vigorously rubbing her hands together.

Norva stood still. 'What *I* did? What did *I* do?'

Norva looked back at me, with panic in her eyes.

I shrugged, but I was intrigued. What did she do?

'That was years ago, Kat – I mean, Katarzyna,' said Pap.

'Oh my god – what did baby Norv do to upset you, TrojKat?' Norva pleaded. 'Whatever it was I am eternally sorry. I was a different person back then! I've changed!'

Katarzyna pursed her lips. A tight-lipped smile grew across her face.

She looked at Pap. 'She doesn't know?'

3

'What doesn't Norv know? Am I about to get some fresh, straight out of the oven gossip?' said a voice behind us. George Shah. 14. Norva's best friend. They laugh together for hours on end. Future music man. TrojKat's other biggest fan.

He leaned in the doorway.

'Norv knows it all, Kat. Don't you, Norv? What Norv doesn't know, isn't worth your time, tbh.' George grinned and stood between Katarzyna and Norva.

He put an arm around each of them. They both immediately squirmed away.

'What – do I smell, or something? What's the matter?'

Katarzyna brushed her hands down her black belted coat.

'That matter is that they don't know that this one –' she pointed at Norva, '– vomited in my hair when she was like two. Properly foul baby. I remember that smell up 'til today. I'll never forget it.'

She wrinkled her nose and shuddered at the memory, glaring at Norva the whole time.

George laughed wildly, bending forward. 'Ha! That's pure jokes! Ah shame, Norva. An iconic tale for the ages, though. Amazing.'

'It wasn't and isn't amazing' said Katarzyna flatly. 'It's grim,'

'Relax, I didn't even think to tell her about it,' said Pap. He smiled. 'She was only two,'

'Yeah, too disgusting,' said Katarzyna.

Even I had to laugh at that. I bit my lip and looked at Norva.

'I'm well sorry,' she said. She looked at the floor. 'I never knew.'

Norva looked heartbroken. I felt a pang of sympathy for her. Annoyance aside, she is my sister after all.

I looked at her face. Her eyes welled with tears. What's that thing grown-ups say? Never meet your idols?

Norva learnt that today.

'Well, now you do. But apology not accepted!' Katarzyna snapped.

Her seriousness silenced the office.

George coughed to break it. He smiled widely at Katarzyna.

'Leave the past in the past, eh? Let's focus on the future – right? he said. 'Speaking of which – seamless segue – I'm so pumped about tomorrow! I can't thank you enough for this experience. Look at me, properly smashing it.' George grinned. 'Beats work experience at Boots, right?'

Katarzyna sighed and slumped against the door frame. 'I suppose.'

'Ayyy, Kat, what you mean 'suppose'? You were properly buzzing about this when we met in July –'

Norva sighed at the mention of July.

July was when George had met Katarzyna at her concert. As their friendship grew, so did Norva's jealousy.

July meant something else to me. Something more painful.

July was when we lost Hugo. So suddenly.

I gulped.

'Yeah, well, things change,' said Katarzyna. 'They change quickly.'

I knew this to be very true. I stared at the floor and took a deep breath.

'Real talk,' said George. At least he agreed with me. 'But this video shoot is going to be incredible – you know that right?'

'For you, maybe,' Katarzyna said quietly.

She tapped her thumbnail against the other fingers of her right hand. She looked away and blinked slowly. She put her sunglasses back on her face.

'You alright?' asked Pap. He reached out to touch her shoulder. She recoiled before he made contact.

'Yeah, yeah, I'm fine. Fine!' She sniffed.

She didn't seem 'fine'. At all.

'It's just weirding me out, being here.'

A valid explanation. Was I sensing a soft, warm heart underneath her cold, hard exterior?

'Well, I'll make sure you have a great time, and give you the homecoming you deserve,' said George softly.

'Homecoming?' she snorted. 'Nah, I don't think so – I'm out. This is going to be the last thing I do. Here on the Tri I mean. Maybe London.'

George stared at her. 'What? Where you going?'

Katarzyna's sighed and waved her hand. 'No, forget it. Ignore me, I'm tired.' She looked at George. 'I appreciate the help, though. I need it.'

Norva looked up.

'Help?' she said, her voice light, fresh and friendly. 'If you need help, I've got loads to give.' She looked at George. 'Maybe we can get involved, too? I can make it up to you, Katarzyna. Me and Nik can do some running –?'

'– I prefer to walk, actually,'

Norva laughed 'Nah sis, "running" means helping out and going to get stuff on fancy film shoots. We can do that! Can't we?'

I shrugged. The gesture was an accurate reflection of my feelings. I did not want to help Katarzyna personally, but, truthfully, I was interested in being close to the action.

'No,' said Katarzyna flatly. 'Not you. Not with your track record'

'But I've changed,' Norva wailed. Like a baby.

That did absolutely nothing to strengthen her case.

'No,' Katarzyna replied firmly. 'I don't need you.'

4

Norva looked at the floor and bit her lip, blinking slowly while she gazed at the concrete. She shook her head and then raised it to look at Katarzyna. She shrugged. 'You might one day,' she said.

Katarzyna rolled her eyes. 'Doubt it,' she snorted.

My suspicion of a presence of a soft, warm heart was evidently incorrect.

'George,' she raised her voice in his direction. 'You want to start now?' she said, but she didn't look at George. She looked at Norva.

She reached into her bag; her eyes remained on Norva. She was evidently very serious about her grudge.

She pulled out her green leather purse and looked through it. 'The crew are incoming – I need supplies.'

Katarzyna waved two £50 notes towards George. I'd never seen one of those before, let alone two.

Neither had Norva. She gasped as Katarzyna pushed them into George's hand. 'Wow – now you're rich too,

George,' she whispered under her breath. George rolled up the notes and put them into the back pocket of his jeans.

'Sissy still on The Tri?' asked Katarzyna.

George nodded. 'Where else is she going to be?'

Katarzyna laughed. 'Of course. Go over to Better Buy and load up on snacks. Popcorn, sparkling water, Hola-Cola, crisps – Oh! Make sure you get a whole load of those Beast Bites. Know the ones?'

George shook his head, but Norva nodded.

'Get all of them, especially the Spicy Beef ones. Afua loves those ones. If Sissy's got special Halloween ones, get them.'

'Hold up, are you not getting a catering truck?' said a clearly-disappointed George. 'I was properly looking forward to that. Just last night I was dreaming about getting my lips around some tacos or whatever munch it would have on its mobile menu. Om nom nom.' He licked his lips.

'Nope,' Katarzyna said. 'No catering – we're making a video, not a scene. I don't want everyone to know I'm here until it's unavoidable.'

'Well, Katarzyna, I don't think that's realistic, I –' started Pap.

It wasn't at all.

Katarzyna raised her hand to stop him. She continued.

'I just don't fancy feeding all these hungry mouths round here. I want to be in and out.'

George nodded. 'Got it, boss.'

I recounted Katarzyna's list in my head. I took out my phone and noted it for permanence.

George kissed his teeth in my direction. 'No need for that, Nik – I got this,' he said.

'You have?' Katarzyna replied. 'Now go get it! Keep the change – and the receipts, OK. It's a business expense.'

Norva looked at me. 'Yeah, we'll make sure he keeps the receipts, alright.'

I smiled. "Receipts" is what Norva calls the evidence we collect for our cases.

I scrolled through Katarzyna's list on my phone.

Spicy Beef Beast Bites – for Afua

'Who's Afua?' I asked, distracting a puzzled Katarzyna.

'Afua Martey. I've known her forever.'

Pap chuckled. 'Ah! I remember Afua – sweet girl. How is she?'

'Alright. She's my manager,' Katarzyna looked at the floor. 'For now, at least.'

'That's really good of you,' said Norva, her words deep-fried in sarcasm. 'You're truly generous – remembering where you came from, helping those around you, sharing your success.'

Pap looked at Norva. He offered her a sympathetic smile.

Ding! Ding!

Katarzyna's phone. She pulled it out of her bag and swiped at the screen.

'That's Afua now – she's on her way.'

Without glancing up at Pap she held out her hand.

Pap chuckled to himself, raised his hands and shook his head. He stood up and went to the wall-mounted gunmetal grey security box. 'Alright,' he said, rifling through the keys. 'These are the ones. Corner Three. Flat 223 and a key to the roof.' Katarzyna reached for the key, but Pap held on to them. He clutched them to his chest.

'Listen – you need to look after the place, OK? The TriAngels – remember them? The charity here at The Tri?'

Katarzyna nodded.

'Well, they're excited – I'm excited – that you've come back to the estate for your video. They are very grateful for your generous donation, of course.'

Katarzyna waved her hand. 'Pocket money.'

Pap rubbed at his neck. 'I'm sure it's going to be great – but look after it. Please? I don't need drama. Your parents told me how messy you used to be.' Pap placed the keys in her hand.

Katarzyna snatched them and pushed them into her bag, no thanks offered.

'So someone still talks to them?' she muttered. 'Good for them.'

Intriguing.

I looked over at Norva. Her head was already titled in anticipation of potential drama.

'Don't talk to them about me anymore, alright? I don't want them to know I'm here,' said Katarzyna.

'Good luck with that,' said Norva. 'That's impossible. You can't keep secrets on The Tri.'

5

Katarzyna and George stepped out of Pap's office. I
waited in the doorway for Norva. She put her backpack
on her shoulders. Pap smiled and gently patted her head.
She smiled up at him. He nodded and sat back at his desk.
He sighed, rubbed his eyes and went back to his screen.
He squinted at it.

He really needed an eye test.

I zipped up my parka and walked past the lift. I pushed
the external doors open. A light breeze hit my face and
went up my nostrils. It drizzled slightly.

Katarzyna and George stood in the darkened doorway.

'Appreciate this, George. See you in the green room,'
Katarzyna said. She pointed up at Corner Three. 'You
know where it is?'

George nodded, and she blew him a kiss.

She looked us up and down. 'Bye,' she said shortly.

She turned, crossed The Tri and was quickly swallowed
by its shadows.

'In a bit, Kat,' George called into the darkness.

'Why is she calling the flat the green room?' I said. 'It's not green – all the flats are painted light yellow around here.'

This was a fact. It's the estate's default paint. Unless you want to pay a premium. Or unless you own your flat outright.

'Yeah, it's funny, right?' said George. 'A green room is basically where crews and artists hang out and get ready before they go on set or on stage, or whatever.'

'Interesting,' I said. 'But why green? I don't understand. It doesn't make sense.'

George shrugged. 'Literally none.' He looked ahead at the shop. 'Listen, gotta run this errand. I'll catch you up in a bit.'

He put his hands in his jacket's pockets and paced quickly towards Better Buy.

'Wait, wait, wait,' said Norva. 'As if you're going shopping without us, G – I'll show her I can be helpful,' said Norva. 'She'll see. Let's go.'

She linked arms with me, and we ran to catch up with him.

'Must spend my millions,' said George. He rubbed his hands together. 'This money is actually burning a hole in my pocket – I can feel its lucrative fire singeing my leg hair, I –'

As we walked, his voice faded out.

I glanced over to the refuse area, gulped and slowed down.

It had been 107 days since Hugo, and every 24 hours still hurt.

Norva noticed my decrease in pace and followed my gaze. She squeezed my arm.

'I know,' she said quietly. 'It's still so rough. But look on the bright side. We have a great distraction, a new adventure. The actual real-life TrojKat is here, and yes maybe she's a bit icy but still…' she raised her voice, '… George has coins, and we get to hang out with a film crew. Think of the glamour, and the gossip!'

She pinched my cheek. I slapped her hand away.

'Who's "we", Norva?' I said. 'She doesn't like us.'

George nodded his head. 'I've got to agree. No glamour for you two,' he said. 'You heard what she said, she isn't interested.' He put his hand on Norva's shoulder. 'Sucks for her though – she'll miss out on all this NSquared goodness.'

"NSquared" was the mathematical duo name George called us – and only George.

'That's right. You stay loyal,' said Norva.

George smiled.

'She says that now, but once she sees how useful we are, she'll switch up that opinion, no doubt about it. That frown will flip all the way around.'

'I don't think so,' I said. 'She seems like a truly terrible person. Sorry George – I know you like her. It's making me question your judgement, if I'm honest.'

He shrugged. 'When are you not honest? I see your point,

though. She's not showing you her best side, that's for sure.'

'Good side, bad side, doesn't matter – we're still in,' said Norva.

'Norv, yo, listen,' said George. 'I know you're the Original Eager Beaver, and I highly respect that energy, but also – hear me out – don't go in too hard and mess this up for me. Kat's already in a funky mood.'

'Yes, she certainly not as nice as you claimed over the summer, George,' I said. 'She's very different.'

'Yeah, major fake news!' said Norva.

In return, George gently pulled on one of Norva's braids. She screamed in theatrical pain.

I rolled my eyes.

'I know Norva is annoying,' I said. 'It's been her default mode for the duration of my existence – but even I believe it's unreasonable to be upset at a baby's misdeeds eleven years after the fact.'

'I don't know,' said Norva, 'I'm pretty mad at me about it.'

George laughed. 'Yeah, I agree,' he said. 'She's changed. She's well different from when I met her in the summer.'

'Why do you think that is?' I asked.

'Errm, that's obvious!' snorted Norva. 'The Arcadia

deal? All the money and fame coming her way? She's now big leagues, big time. Honestly, I wouldn't want to hang around with plebs like us either. I can't hate her for that.'

'You're colder than February,' laughed George.

Norva shrugged. 'I'm just keeping it real.'

'Yeah, real dumb,' said George. 'But yeah, since the ink hit the paper on that contract, she's not the same.'

'She's just leaning into her new next-level vibe. She can't be the same old nice humble person. She has to dial it up.'

'That sounds a lot like fraud, Norva.' I said.

'It's not fraud, it's just the way it is. You gotta to switch it up to get anywhere. Take Pap's phone voice: same guy, different tone.'

She had a point.

'I suppose.'

'I don't "suppose", I know,' she laughed. 'Trust me on this – how do you think I function?"

6

Better Buy was covered in fake cobwebs.

A pumpkin sat in the window. Its carving was mostly indecipherable.

I was 85% sure it was a pumpkin, carved on a pumpkin.

Meta. Pumpkinception.

On the glass, a poorly applied sticker of the silhouette of a witch on a broomstick pointed towards the shop's sign.

'Festive,' said Norva.

George pushed the door. The little bell rang.

We stepped into the store.

'Hello girls, and George!' Sissy sang from behind the till.

Sissy St Claire. 60. Loose lips, never zipped. 'Do you like what I've done with the store?' she said.

'Yeah!' said George. 'It's well spooky, I'm scared to even shop here now! Wow Sissy - dial it down!'

George. Always eager to please. Always so enthusiastic.

'Don't lie George, it's basic,' said Norva. She walked to the end of store. 'It is a bit satanic, though. What would Jesus do?' She shouted back down the aisle. 'What would he *think*, Sissy? What would he *say*?'

Norva. The opposite of George.

Sissy clutched at her chest. I reached for Norva's arm.

'Norva, you have to be nicer to Sissy. She's apologised to us for what she said about Pap over the summer. Let it go.'

'Nah, never,' said Norva with a scowl. 'Plus, holding a grudge is jokes. It gives me life. Go get a basket.'

'I'm not your gopher, Norva. I don't go-for this or go-for that.'

Norva laughed. 'Love that, love it – but get me a basket. Please.'

I sighed. I walked to the front of the store. I gave Sissy an apologetic half-smile. She smiled back.

'Looking forward to Halloween?' she asked quietly.

'Not at all,' I replied.

I caught up with Norva and George.

Norva's hands were already filled with snacks. 'Great, keep holding it.' She threw her shopping into the basket.

'Hey, George,' she said. 'Look at us. Hey, look at us. Helping you help Kat. Who would've thought?'

'Not me,' said George. 'I'm lying, I knew you'd muscle in somehow. But this is where it ends, yeah?'

Norva laughed. 'Yeah, right,' she said.

I peered into the basket.

- Buttermist Popcorn – sweet. Three packets. Each 90 grams
- Buttermist Popcorn – salted. Four packets. Each 90 grams
- Buttermist Popcorn – sweet and salted. Three packets. Each 90 grams

To the basket, I added:

Beast Bites – Spooky Spicy Beef. 10 packets. Each 30 grams

'For Afua,' I said.

'Well remembered,' George said with a smile.

'Told you; we're essential,' said Norva. 'NSquared are a necessity.'

At the fridge. Norva added:

- Nevian Water – still –. two x two litres
- Don Petrofino Water – sparkling – two x two litres

'Wait, wait, wait – don't crush the snacks,' said George. He tapped his forehead. 'Think about what you're doing.' He ran to get another basket. He smiled at Sissy and gave her two thumbs up.

'Such a suck up, that one,' said Norva.

'Do we need all this?' he said when he returned.

'Of course you do,' said Norva. 'You need it all.'

7

George's basket contained:

- Hola-Cola – Regular, two litres.
- Hola-Cola – Diet, two litres.
- Hola-Cola – NulCal, two litres.

'What's even the difference between Diet and NulCal?' asked George.

'Nothing but branding,' said Norva. 'But it works on me.'

'I don't know how much longer I can hold this basket, Norva,' I said.

My right humerus threatened to bid goodbye to my scapula and go home.

'Don't be a baby. We're done.'

The door to the shop opened. The little bell rang, and Norva ran to the till. 'Yep, they'll appreciate this!' she said, picking up a tiny plastic pumpkin. 'Spooky Season demands it.'

She flicked its light on and off.

I carried my basket to the till. Every second and step hurt.

George struggled with his behind us.

Norva did not struggle. No. She played with the pumpkin, laughing at its illumination.

I put my basket on the floor, while Sissy served someone at the till.

Someone we didn't recognise.

Approximately 180 centimetres tall. Pale white skin. Short blonde hair. Hazel eyes. Blue jeans. Buying five newspapers and three bags of Beast Bites. Spooky Spicy Beef.

Norva stood on tip toes behind me. She cast an eye over the man's shopping. She gave me a confused look.

'Those snacks are so hot right now,' she whispered. 'And why so many papers?'

'At the end of the day, too,' I said. 'Papers are a resource for mornings.'

'Archaic,' Norva said in a low voice. 'Hey, Old News!' she said, louder. 'Old News, hey!'

She got his attention.

'Mate – who buys newspapers when Twitter exists?' she laughed. George joined in.

The man looked at Norva.

'It's more real this way,' he said. He handed his money over to Sissy.

Norva stared at the man.

'I'm glad someone's buying *The New York Witness*,' said Sissy. 'I get a copy everyday, and it mostly never sells. This is the last time I stock it.'

'Great,' said the man. He didn't look up.

I craned my neck to look at the paper. Its title was written in large thick old English-style decorated letters.

He walked to the door. He put his change and his receipt into his back pocket.

The coins slipped in easily, but the small slip of paper hung from his pocket for two seconds. It fell to the floor.

I reached out and grabbed it.

He opened the door. The little bell rang.

'Excuse me, you've –' I began to say, but he was gone.

I folded the receipt and put it into my pocket.

Norva smiled. 'That's right. Keep that for the files.'

'Ready for us, Sissy?' asked George.

She nodded. 'Come on, blessed ones.'

Norva and George threw our shopping onto the counter.

Sissy pushed her wheelchair back.

She looked at us, and back at our shopping.

Norva blinked at her until she wheeled herself back to

her till.

Between scanning the items, Sissy looked us up and down.

'£35.45 please,' she said. 'That's a lot of money to spend on snacks, do your parents —'

'Let me stop you right there,' said Norva.

She snatched a £50 note from George's hand and slapped it down onto the counter.

'Yes, they know.'

8

The three of us stood outside Better Buy.

18:41.

Eight plastic bags between us.

Every one of them heavy.

The orange light from the pumpkin flashed on and off, in the bag closest to my right foot.

'Well – night George,' said Norva. 'Have a great night with Kat, send her kisses from us.'

She grabbed my arm, turned and walked away. She chuckled under her breath.

'Oi, what?' said George. 'Wait! Norv, wait! Nik, tell her! You can't leave me out here struggling like this!'

Norva stopped walking. Our backs to him.

'What do you mean?' she said. She smiled widely at me. 'Have fun with your new friends. Let us know how it goes. Updates in real time, please.'

'Nah, Norva – come on now. You've properly stitched me up here! How am I going to carry all of this over to

Corner Three by myself?'

'Oh, do you need help?' she asked. 'Isn't this where our help ends?'

George threw his hands up. 'You scammer – I should have clocked you in the shop – getting so much stuff so you could get up there.' He shook his head. 'I'm fully outraged! Outraged!'

'No you're not – you're impressed. Don't lie,' she said.

Ding! Ding!

George's phone. He rummaged in his pocket for it.

'Ahh, no, it's Kat!'

'What does the message say?' I asked.

'What do you think?' snorted Norva. 'She's ringing the bell for her little butler. Right, George?'

He put his phone back in his pocket.

'Just help me please?' George pleaded. 'Just to the door.'

'Pffft,' said Norva. 'No deal.'

'I'll even split some of the change with you.'

'Getting warmer,' said Norva. 'Three-way split?'

He sighed. 'Yeah.'

'And you promise you'll put in a good word for us?'

'Fine!'

'Deal!'

George and Norva shook hands.

George picked up three bags. So did Norva. I reached for the last two.

We walked across The Tri.

'Can't you put some of this in your backpack?' I asked Norva.

'Yeah!' said George. 'Why are we here struggling when you could be doing way more?'

'Pfft,' said Norva. She looked over her shoulder. 'This bag is for style and creating opportunities only, not for carrying bulky stuff. Get real.'

George kissed his teeth. I shook my head. We kept walking.

Coins jangled in George's pocket behind me.

'That's a lot of change, George,' I said. 'I can't believe she gave you so much money.'

'Same!' he said. 'Even though she said keep it all, I can't keep like sixty pounds.'

'£64.55,' I said.

'Well you're not keeping all of it, are you? We're taking our cut, and that's that on that,' said Norva. 'Nik, run the numbers, what are we getting?'

'£21.52 each – well, one of us gets £21.51.'

'And that one is George,' said Norva with a laugh.

George dropped his bags and leaned against the wall of Corner Three. He winced and flexed his fingers. 'Fine, it's fine – get money.' He reached into his pocket and gave Norva the remaining fifty pound note. 'Kat actually likes me – and that's priceless. Coins can't buy you that kind of clout.'

Norva swung a bag at his leg. 'Shut it,' she snapped. She snatched at the money. 'Thanks! But don't remind her of the change. Hopefully she'll forget.'

'I wouldn't forget about £64.55,' I said. 'Not at all.'

'Well, she's not at all like you, is she? She's not living any kind of low-budget life like us.'

'Not now, maybe. But she did live here for most of her life, Norva. She's a lot like us. More than she'd like to admit, I'm sure.'

Norva shrugged.

I put both my bags in my left hand and opened the door to the lobby of Corner Three with my right.

'George, what exactly are you doing on the shoot, anyway?' I asked.

'Sound, of course.'

Of course, sound.

Music is everything to George.

'Well, I'm shadowing someone – working with this guy

Simon. He was at the gig where I met them all. He's an old mate of Kat's from college. He's showing me how to level up, get professional. Properly cool guy.'

'So you'll have access to all the audio from the shoot?' I said.

'Yep,'

'And you'll be sending us snippets for our files?' said Norva.

'Nope,' said George.

'I spoke too soon when I called you loyal, didn't I?'

George laughed.

I pushed the button for the lift.

9

The three tall thin towers on The Triangle Estate are identical. We call them Corners.

We live in Corner One. George and his mother live there too, on the floor below us. The 21st.

Each Corner has:
- 22 floors
- 66 flats – three per floor
- one lift
- one staircase

We took the lift to the top floor.

This lift looked exactly the same as the one we used every day in Corner One – but it somehow felt different.

Unfamiliar.

Norva says the Corners have 'same skins, but different souls.'

I understood what she meant.

What would Hugo would call it? I thought. Yes. 'Uncanny.' That's what he used to say.

I sighed.

I missed him so much.

I looked around the lift. My eye was drawn to its pulsating light.

It cast trembling shadows across George and Norva's faces. They made eerie expressions at each other to its rhythm.

'Imagine if this light was red?' Norva said.

'Would be too spooky for me!' laughed George.

I sniffed the air. I grimaced. Norva laughed.

'Unfresh, right?' she said.

I nodded.

George agreed. 'I'd get it in summer – everyone smells ripe in the heat – but now, in autumn?' said George. 'Corner Threes roll different. Someone definitely peed in here. Recently.'

The lift shuddered to a halt.

'I wonder if their view up here on 22 is as good as ours,' said Norva.

We stepped out of the lift.

'You know what? No! I don't think that. What I do think is that you're being unprofessional.'

Katarzyna hissed down her phone.

She stood outside flat 223.

Her back to us.

'Are you in this or not? Because you're not acting like you want to be!'

Norva silently placed her bags on the floor. She grabbed my arm and pushed me back against the wall.

She put her fingers to her lips. I rolled my eyes. Of course I was going to be quiet.

She turned to George and covered his mouth. He nodded.

'I know that – yes. Yes! You've said that. Hmmm. Yep. Yes. I get that. I told *you* that. I know you're trying, I get that… but think about the bigger picture here. You're thinking too small. There's a plan. We have a plan. Remember? Stick to it.'

I looked up at Norva. My narrowed eyes said:


```
Who is Katarzyna talking to?
```


Norva shrugged.

Katarzyna ended her phone call abruptly. She sighed deeply – it was more of a growl, actually – and stuffed her phone into her pocket. Norva picked up her bags. She nudged George forward and we stepped out.

'Yeah, there's no way you could have carried this all by yourself, George – I hope Katarzyna doesn't mind us being here,' Norva said. Her saccharine skills on show.

She nudged me with her elbow and narrowed her eyes.

'Yes, I'm sure Ms Clarke won't mind us helping George. We are such good helpers,' I said flatly.

I smiled at her sarcastically.

Norva gave me an exasperated look in return.

Katarzyna spun around. The wide smile on her face quickly fell. 'About time, George.' She looked down at our bags, and up at our faces. 'Thanks for helping him, I guess,' she said through pursed lips.

'Not a problem,' I replied. 'George has some change for you, Katarzyna. £64.55.'

Norva kicked my left ankle. George kicked my right.

Katarzyna swatted the air. 'Don't care. He can keep it. Actually, he should give you some. A tip,' she chuckled to herself.

Norva beamed. 'Thank you!'

'Whatever.' She reached for the keys in her pocket. As she put them in the door, she paused before turning them.

'Everything alright?' asked Norva.

'Fine. Absolutely stellar,'

Kat bit her bottom lip, and her eyes were moist.

10

Corner Three. Flat 223.

Exactly the same layout as ours.

Bedroom at the front by the door. A bathroom. Another bedroom. Its door was closed. From the hall you could see into the living room and hear movement.

'You want the bags in the kitchen?' asked Norva.

Katarzyna nodded but didn't look up from her phone. 'Unpack them and go. I don't want you here longer than necessary.'

Norva sighed.

We each picked up two bags and walked them to the kitchen, through the living room. Just like we would at home.

The living room was furnished but basic. Incredibly basic:

- a sofa, black
- a table, four chairs

That was it. Not homely. Not glamorous. Not fit for the superstar I was told that Katarzyna was.

Norva removed her backpack. She placed it next to the table. She glanced around the room quickly. She made eye contact with George and me. She kicked her bag beneath the table and smiled. She raised her thumbs.

George and I looked at each other.

I shook my head at Norva. 'Pick that up!' I whispered.

Norva put her fingers in her ears and turned away to face the bags on the worktop. She rifled through the bags and found the plastic pumpkin. She turned it on and placed it on the kitchen counter.

'That's better,' she said. 'Ambience.'

The closed bedroom door opened.

A tall thin man. Approximately 186 centimetres. Light brown skin. Curly black hair. Thick black glasses. Some kind of fluffy grey scarf around his neck as he stepped into the living room.

'Yes, yes – Simon Brook!' said George. 'How do?' George dropped his bags and rushed over to high-five him. George turned to Norva and I. 'This is the sound guy I was talking about. Get it? 'Sound' guy? Because he works on sounds and he's also cool as ice?'

Simon laughed.

'Alright George?' Simon replied. He turned to us. 'Hi,' he

extended his hand. I shook it.

I looked at Simon's face. He looked familiar.

'Have we met?' I said.

Norva narrowed her eyes. 'Yeah, who are you? You've been on The Tri before, haven't you?'

'Yeah – I have – I used to work in journalism.'

That's it. Face placed.

'Oh yeah!' said Norva. 'You used to work with that mean May lady from Cloud News, didn't you?'

'I did, yeah,' said Simon. 'Glad to be out of it too.'

'Yeah, she ain't right,' said Norva. 'Nothing but bad vibes.'

I looked at Simon's neck. 'I like your scarf,' I said. 'It's interesting.'

'Oh this? This isn't a scarf,' said Simon, removing it from his neck. 'This is a cover for the microphone we're using tomorrow.'

'And what a sick microphone it is!' said George. 'You can hear people walking on the moon with that thing, it's no joke. I need one in my life on a full-time basis.'

A knock at the door.

Katarzyna paced quickly down the hall.

'Where you been, Afua?' she said, opening the door.

The Afua Martey. Katarzyna's manager and old friend. Dark brown skin. Long, thick dreads. Short, square body. She walked down the hall into the living room.

'Tube, overground, bus, Kat.' Afua said. 'It was the longest.'

She looked past Katarzyna. 'Alright Simon?' Simon nodded.

'George!' she said. She looked at us, and back at George. 'These your girlfriends?'

I recoiled. I would never be George's girlfriend. Anyone's girlfriend.

'Haha, nah nah!' George laughed. 'They're my friends: Norva's my bestie and Nik is her sister,' said George.

'And they're going. Now.' said Katarzyna. 'I told you not to come here, Norva.'

'Norva, eh?' said Afua narrowing her eyes. She widened them quickly. 'Oh yeah! I've heard all about *you*! You're that baby that puked in Kat's hair back in the day. Jokes! She's still not over it you know?'

'Yes. I know,' said Norva. She stared at the floor.

I felt a pang of sympathy for her.

'Ha! Haha!' laughed Afua. 'That was hilarious, I had to wash her hair like nine times to get the smell out. What were your parents feeding you, damn? I mean, really.'

Afua turned to Simon. 'This was before your time, Si – before sixth form.'

'I've heard the story, though,' said Simon, smiling.

'Eurgh, I'm actually over this,' said Norva. 'I –'

Another knock at the door.

11

'We're leaving,' said Norva. I noticed that her eyes were wet. I felt another pang of pity for Norva.

'Good,' said Katarzyna. 'Get the door on your way out, yeah?'

'Norv –' George began. Norva shook her head. She put her hand up to stop him speaking. 'Catch up with you later?'

George nodded.

Norva walked down the hallway. I followed behind her. She opened the door.

Someone we recognised stood in the doorframe. 180 centimetres approximately. Pale white skin. Short blonde hair. Hazel eyes. Blue jeans.

The man from Better Buy.

A small carrier bag in his left hand. A case on wheels behind him with his right hand.

'Interesting,' said Norva! 'Look, it's Old News.' '

I think I've got the wrong flat,' he said. He stepped out

of the door frame and looked down the corridor back towards the lift.

'No,' said Norva. 'You're looking for Katarzyna, right? This is the place.'

'Ah, OK, good,' he replied.

'I didn't know you were part of the team?' I said.

He looked at me.

'Why would you? I don't know you.' He pushed passed us. The wheels of his case ran over Norva's foot. 'Excuse me,' said Norva. She narrowed her eyes in his direction.

She followed him. I followed her. We loitered in the hallway.

'Team!' he said brightly to the room. 'Hi James!' said Katarzyna and Afua. Cheerfully, in unison.

Simon nodded. 'Hi.'

'Saw these and thought of you, Afua, even though they're gross,' he said.

He reached into his bag. He pulled out a bag of Beast Bites – Spooky Spicy Beef – and threw them at her.

She caught them deftly.

'Yas! These are the best,' Afua said. She immediately opened the snack. 'Tasty!'

The pungent smell instantly filled the room. I recoiled. Hideous.

'We bought some for you, too,' Norva said. 'In the

kitchen.'

'What do you mean you bought some too, you're not part of the shoot are you?' said James.

He turned to Afua. 'Afua. Cancel this, no more kids on set. Liabilities. One is enough.' He looked at George.

'Nothing to do with me, mate,' Afua licked her fingers and put her hands up. 'These are George's stragglers.'

'We're no one's stragglers.' said Norva to Afua. Norva stood up straight. 'Who are you anyway?' she said to James.

'This' said Katarzyna dramatically, 'is James Paul Dean.' 'The best in the business.'

Katarzyna looked at James and smiled.

He smiled warmly back at her.

'James Paul Dean?' snorted Norva. 'That's your name? Three bland first names chucked together? Gosh, your parents were low-effort.'

Afua burst out laughing. 'Right?' she laughed. Her mouth full of Beast Bites. 'That's what I said when I met him! Funny. Funny!'

'Norva, stop,' said George in a low whisper.

Norva shrugged. James smiled, but it didn't reach his eyes.

'Just James is fine. I'm actually named after the film star – you know the one from the 50s?'

'I don't,' said Norva. 'What took you so long, anyway?'

'What do you mean?' said Katarzyna. She raised an eyebrow.

'Well, we've been here for a while now –' said Norva.

'Unfortunately,' said Katarzyna.

'– and he was ahead of us in the shop. Where's your reading materials?'

'Reading materials?' said Afua. 'What are they on about, James?'

'He bought five newspapers,' I said.

James laughed. 'Observant,' he said. He looked at us. 'Reviews. *Expedition: Intolerable* came out today. I did the wire work –'

I wondered what wire work was. Was James Paul Dean an electrician?

'– I wanted to know what the world thinks – it was a big one for me.'

Afua cheered. 'Ayyy, nice work.'

Simon was silent.

Katarzyna looked into James's eyes. 'This should "catapult" you to the big leagues,' she said.

'Hope so,' he replied with a smile I hadn't seen before.

A smile seemly reserved for Katarzyna and for Katarzyna alone.

'Where are they though?' asked Norva looking at his

hands and around his body. 'Your papers?'

'What's with you two and your questions?' asked Afua. 'You're well nosy. Answer them though, James. I'm invested in this mystery now.'

James dropped his case and walked to the fridge. He leaned on the kitchen counter. He picked up the plastic pumpkin and turned it off.

Norva sighed.

'The papers are in the car,' he said. 'I went to get additional equipment for tomorrow, double check I had spare carabiner clips and ropes. This is a big one for her.' He stared at Katarzyna. 'I need to make sure she is safe. Her safety is everything to me.'

Ah – James Paul Dean was a stuntman.

Katarzyna stared at James. 'Thanks, James,' she said breathlessly.

Afua choked on her snack. She coughed into the room. Maize-based snack particles shot from her mouth.

'You should really cover your mouth when you do that,' I said. 'It's impolite.'

The group turned and looked at me.

'Get out,' Afua said.

'We're going, we're going,' said Norva.

She pulled on my arm and we walked to the door.

Ding! Ding!

James reached into his pocket.

'It's Hester – she's lost. She's found that pub downstairs and wants us to meet her there.'

'No. No pub!' said Katarzyna. 'I told you all – I don't want people to know I'm here. I don't need it.'

'Oh, come on, Kat,' said Afua. 'We have been summoned by the great director herself, Hester Bos. It'll be fine!'

I saw Kat's expression, and knew that she disagreed.

12

Lifts on The Tri claimed they held ten people, but this one felt tight with seven occupants.

We squeezed in. Katarzyna squashed between Simon and James.

Katarzyna tutted loudly. 'Look at my life,' she muttered under her breath.

'A TrojKat Sandwich – only available on The Tri!' Katarzyna sighed.

The lift's light flickered across us.

Afua laughed loudly, close to my face.

The smell of Beast Bites filled the lift. This, layered on top of the pre-existing smell of urine, was foul.

'It's not funny, Afua,' Katarzyna snapped. 'We should have taken two trips. It stinks in here and I'm squashed.'

Yes and yes. I agreed with her on both of her points.

'No, too long – Hester's waiting,' said James.

'Yeah, he's right that would have taken ages, you said it yourself,' said Afua. 'You know how long these lifts are.'

Please stop talking, Afua. I couldn't take the smell. Was this how managers behaved? She was acting barely older than Norva.

I held my breath, but Afua should have been holding hers.

I counted the floors as they passed by to distract myself. As we went down, Katarzyna sung for her sardine audience.

We're living at the cusp
Existing by the brink
What happens if we swim?
Do I sink?
When every day you rise
Do you watch me fall?
You look back while you run
And see me crawl

I recognised those lyrics. That was the song Norva had been attempting to sing in Pap's office.

Of course she was.

To my credit, though, Katarzyna version was much stronger. Clearer. It was actually good. 7/10. George and Norva clapped next to my ears.

'You can stop clapping, Norva,' said Katarzyna.

I moved my head closer to Afua.

'Pretty good acoustics in here,' said Afua.

A wave of Spicy Beef Bites hit my face.

I recoiled. Too much. Way too much.

'Please stop,' I whispered.

'What?' said Afua. 'What's wrong with you?'

'The smell of those snacks – I can't take it. They're disgusting.'

Afua flung her orange-stained fingers to her mouth.

'It's not personal, it's just the snacks,' I said through tight lips.

'Cut the dramatics,' snapped Katarzyna. 'We've only got three floors to go – we're basically there now.'

The lift stopped with a shudder.

I jabbed at the open button.

'Girl, calm down, you know that button is dead and redundant, like the ones on The Tube. Let it do its thing,' said Afua, still her hand covering her mouth.

I jabbed again at the button and pushed through the lift door as it slowly creaked open.

I leaned against the wall of the lobby. Fresh air. I gulped it down.

'You alright?' asked Simon, his hand on my shoulder.

I squirmed away from his touch. 'Yes, fine,' I said. 'Those snacks just stink.'

'I totally get it,' he laughed. 'They're pretty disgusting.'

I nodded. He looked up at the group, who were walking quickly in the direction of Bermuda's – the bar on The Tri.

In the distance I heard Afua kissing her teeth. James laughed deeply while Katarzyna rubbed hand sanitizer on her palms.

'Well, it was nice to meet you,' said Simon. 'I'm going to catch up with the others.'

He smiled down on me. I gave a slight smile in return. He was certainly friendlier than the others.

He looked at George. 'And I'll see you in the morning – take care of your friend.'

'Will do,' said George.

13

'Well, that whole thing up there, and getting the lift down here was an entire hot mess,' said Norva. She shook her head.

I breathed deeply. 'Too many people, too small a space.'

I shuddered. I should have taken the stairs.

'Now they think both of us are babies, though!' Norva leaned against the wall. 'We're going to need to find another angle to get on this shoot.'

I looked over at Norva. 'Another angle, Norva? They've been rude to you since we've met them? Why do you still want to be part of it?'

'I know, I know – and it stings. They were cutting me real deep up there, but, you know, the FOMO is real.'

'FOMO?' I asked. 'What's FOMO?'

'Fear Of Missing Out,' said George. 'All Norva needs is a formal diagnosis, because she's got all the symptoms.'

Norva nodded. 'And getting on the set will be my cure.'

'But they're terrible people, Norva,' I said. 'This is not worth it.'

'Well Simon's awesome to be fair, and so is Kat – or at least she was before she signed her contract,' said George. 'And look, I still think you're the coolest, Norva, so I'll give you all the gossip from the shoot. Live, direct, in real time. I promise.'

'It's a solid offer, George,' said Norva. 'And one I appreciate – but I want to be fully in. We're getting on that shoot. Let's peek into Bermuda's to see what they're up to.'

'We're not allowed in there,' I said to Norva. 'It's illegal at this time.' I checked my phone. 19:32. It was. Thirty-two minutes too late.

'I didn't say anything about going in, did I?' said Norva.

We walked across The Tri in the dark, using the light from our phones to avoid any piles of poo that may have laid on our path.

'Just so you know, none of this is Ringo's, we would never,' said Norva to George. Ringo. Our dog. Short white hair. Short strong legs. Short snappy temper. I looked up at Corner One, knowing there was a 100% chance Ringo was up there, snoring and sighing.

We reached Bermuda's.

Glasses clinked. Laughter in sync.

We peeked through its perpetually broken window. Norva's and George's heads knocked against each other.

'Watch it, will you?' they said in unison.

'Jinx!' Again, in unison.

They laughed and moved away from the shattered pane.

I stepped forward and spotted the group. They were in various locations across the bar.

Simon sat at a table opposite Afua, talking animatedly at her. She nodded into her phone, paying Simon no attention. She looked up, sighed at the scene at the bar. She smiled at Simon and quickly returned to her phone.

I looked at the bar. Katarzyna was stationed there. People swarmed her like bees. She smiled broadly. Residents buzzed in a meandering queue around her to take photographs. Katarzyna took their phones from them, making sure the angles were just right.

The residents were grateful and delighted.

They hugged her. They patted her back. They kissed her cheeks. Afua had left Simon and stood next to her, beaming proudly.

'There she is,' said George. 'There's the real Kat.'

'Where was that energy for us?' said Norva.

'Missing in action,' I said.

Katarzyna turned away to face the bar. Her face fell. She wiped her cheek in disgust. She reached in her bag for her hand sanitiser.

'There she is,' I said. 'There's the real Katarzyna.'

At the end of a larger table filled with Tri residents, James sat with a woman.

Black bobbed hair. Dark red lips. Luminous white skin.

Two tall glasses with clear liquid stood between them.

The woman's face was still while she talked. She spoke a long, uninterrupted stream of words at James.

She didn't break eye contact.

He stared back at her, his shoulders rising with each sentence he heard.

She reached out to touch his hand. He snatched his away, knocking over the glasses.

He stood up. He said something close to the woman's ear.

He walked to the bar and joined Katarzyna.

He didn't look back.

14

'Who do you reckon that woman is?' said George. 'That vampire-looking one chatting up James Paul Dean?'

'The "vampire-looking one"?' laughed Norva. 'That's a strong, iconic, timeless look, have some respect.'

'She's looks like she's in dress rehearsal costume for tomorrow,' said George.

'I would respect her energy if she was,' said Norva. 'Prepared vibes.'

I sighed. 'The evidence points to that being Hester Bos, the director of the shoot,' I said. 'James received a message from her. The team were meeting her at Bermuda's. That must be who she is.'

'Agree,' said Norva. 'Also, did you sense some hot tension between them? Fire. My waters tell me they used to be a thing, but James is over it now. George, you are so lucky getting a front row seat to this drama. I'm jealous. I hate you.'

The lift doors opened. Norva and George jumped in. I stepped in behind them.

George pushed buttons 21 and 22.

The door closed in front of us.

'Look, NSquared, I'm sorry this one didn't work out for you –'

'That's what you think,' said Norva quietly. She slapped my hand and winked.

George continued. 'It's big sads, truly – but I have to say, I'm buzzing about tomorrow.'

'I'm seething,' said Norva. 'But who could blame you? Not me. You are truly blessed,' said Norva. 'You'll still put in a good word for us, right?'

'Of course,' said George. 'Was going to – am going to.'

'All the kids at school will be shook when you tell them about it at school,' said Norva. '

'They're going to straight-up die of jealousy,' George laughed.

The lift shuddered to a stop. Floor 21.

'This is me!' said George. He bounded out of the lift. 'I'm catching the earliest of nights, I need to be fresh tomorrow. Can't let Trojie down.'

'Trojie?' Norva laughed. 'A nickname for a stage name? Too much!'

'Says you, Norva. You're the one with a dog that

answers to a thousand names – just saying.'

She put her hand to her chest. 'I feel seen,' she replied. 'Night.'

When we unlocked the door to our flat, The Dog That Answers To A Thousand Names didn't stir. We flicked on the light and walked down the hallway. Ringo was in the living room, curled on the sofa. He looked up at us, sighed and went back to sleep.

No Pap.

We checked our phones. 19:46.

No messages.

Norva typed out a message to him.

?????

Pap replied immediately.

Sorry, sorry, at Jane's. Dinner in the fridge – be back soon! xx

Norva threw her phone on the sofa, narrowly avoiding Ringo.

He snarled and bared his teeth at her.

'He's so annoying,' she said, looking in the fridge.

I wasn't sure if she was talking about Pap or Ringo.

Possibly both.

'Rice and peas?'

I nodded and opened the microwave.

15

After dinner – and television – Norva closed the door to our room. 21:47.

She put her hand in her jeans pocket and pulled out the £50 note.

'I'm spending this tomorrow; I'm going to soup up my costume.'

'You're not,' I said. 'Half of it is mine, it's going in the pot for our trip to the Peaks.'

A forthcoming school trip. Pap said going up North would be a good experience for us.

We'll see.

'But that's not until spring next year!' she wailed. 'You know how long that is?'

'137 days,' I said.

'Yeah, ages,' she said. 'But I hear you, I'll keep it.'

Norva got on her bed.

She threw the three jumpers and a pair of jeans that were on it to the floor: She sat cross-legged on her duvet.

She pulled out her phone. Tinny music filled our small space. A now-familiar voice. TrojKat. Norva closed her eyes.

I plugged my phone into its charger.

I looked out of the window.

Norva loudly sung the lyrics.

The night is inky black
But I'm reaching for the light
I'm never looking back
I'll put up a fight

'I'll fight you if you're not quiet, Norva,' I said.

'Leave me alone – I'm getting in the mood for tomorrow,' she said. 'Getting in the zone.'

'For what? We're not going.'

'We are. I'll find a way. Love finds a way.'

'What does that mean?

'I'm not sure, to be honest, I just like how it sounds,'

Norva rolled over and got up. She joined me at the window.

'Before you start – yeah, I know you hate Halloween, I know all about your feelings on it, but look –' she pointed. 'How great does it make The Tri look in the dark? Come on now, give me that!'

She had a point. Orange, green and red lights glowed in windows across the other two towers, creating random, yet predictable patterns.

'It's a bit like Connect 4,' I said.

Norva laughed. 'Yeah it is a bit. I love that game. What a classic.'

She leaned over to look in our telescope. 'It's even better close-up.'

'Magnified.'

'Whatever.'

She moved the telescope to the right, and then down. She pointed it towards the cars parked opposite Bermuda's.

'Well, well, well,' she chuckled. 'Check this out.'

I craned my neck to look.

'Smoking should be banned,' I said.

'I know, right? In this era, anyone who smokes is a real donkey,' said Norva. 'But that's not what I'm scoping, sis. Look closer!'

I moved the telescope approximately one tiny millimetre to the left.

I saw it. I saw them.

Katarzyna and James.

Kissing. Between two cars.

'Oh,' I said.

'Oh?' said Norva, 'Oh? That's your reaction to this development?'

Hand me my phone, I gotta tell George.'

'Let him sleep, Norva,' I said. 'He wanted an early night – let him have one.'

'Who are you? Pap? This is gossip gold! A love triangle on The Tri; with famous people. James and Hester used to be a thing, but now it's James and Kat! This is epic. Epic. If George doesn't know what he's looking at, how can he tell us what he's seeing, if you see what I mean?'

'I don't,' I replied.

Norva pulled my phone from the wall. The charger came with it. She put my phone to her ear. The charger dangled by her chin.

'Gah, he's not answering!'

She threw my phone on the floor.

'Charge it, please.' I said.

'Yeah, yeah,' she replied. She plugged it back into the wall.

Norva curled into bed and sighed.

16

I woke up to Norva's face directly over mine. 10:17.

'Happy Halloween, baby!' she lisped. Fake fangs had replaced her teeth.

'No,' I said. I rolled over.

'You're trash,' she replied.

Bloop! Bloop!

My phone. 5% battery.

'Norva!' I said. 'I specifically asked you to plug my phone back in!'

'I did,' said Norva. At least that's what I think she said. Her news teeth were sliding around her mouth.

'Well it's not charged!' I said. 'I have to charge my phone every night, Norva. You know that!'

I forced it back into the wall. No light or sound to confirm the connection.

'Norva – you must have broken it when you pulled it out the wall so roughly.'

'Throw it here.'

I threw it at her. Hard.

She cupped her hands together and caught it.

'Ok, calm down,' she said.

She attached it to the charger on the desk.

'I can't believe you! Don't use my phone again – use your own!' I blinked angrily at the ceiling.

'Pfft,' said Norva. She took out her teeth. 'It's no big deal, it'll be done charging in no time.'

Oooooh Oooooh

'What's that noise?' I asked.

'It's a ghost! Boo!' she laughed. 'Nah, it's my spooky season text tone, you like?'

'No, I don't like it,' I said. 'I also don't like how your phone is charged – and mine's not.'

'It's George, he's sorry he missed your call last night.'

Oooooh Oooooh

Another message.

'He's not at the flat, yet. Can't talk – family drama.'

Norva paused. 'Family drama? What's that mean?' She

sighed. 'We should just go up to the green room instead of him. This is our moment.'

'It's not our moment, Norva, and we shouldn't just go. I couldn't if I wanted to anyway,' I pointed to my phone.

'Eurgh, you're so annoying,' she said. She sat on her bed, defeated.

'Girls! Food!' shouted Pap.

'Yes!' said Norva. She sprang to her feet. She picked up an orange jumper from the floor. 'Get up,' she said. She hopped on one leg while she put on her jeans. 'By the time we get this food down us, your phone will be plenty charged, and we can roll out.'

She threw a red jumper of hers at me. 'Put this on. Change later.'

I sighed at the ceiling.

I sat up and got dressed. I went to the bathroom and brushed my teeth.

Our table in the living room was filled with Halloween-themed food. Why me?

- Pancakes – bat-shaped
- Boiled eggs – peeled with ghostly faces painted on them
- Toast – shaped like spiderwebs
- Strawberry jam – extra blood-like

Pap stood triumphantly next to the table.

'You look festive,' he said, looking at our red and orange jumpers.

'Don't, Pap,' I said. I shook my head.

Jane Cooper. 42. Chatty. Cheery. Pap's partner. She wiped a plate by the sink and passed it to him. She looked over her shoulder and smiled at us.

'What, do you like live here now?' said Norva, with a sigh.

Jane's face fell.

'Norva!' said Pap.

'I'm sorry, where are my manners? This looks fantastic, Pap,' she smiled. 'And thanks, Jane.' Norva's smile dimmed.

We sat down to eat.

While the theme of the food was definitely not my style, the taste certainly was.

'This is really good,' I said to Jane. The truth. 'And the theme is really… fun.' The lie.

'So pleased you like it,' said Jane. She smiled broadly. 'I just thought you'd like a special Halloween breakfast, I know you love it so much, and –'

Ding! Ding!

74

We all reached for our phones, before I remembered mine was still in our room.

It was Pap's. He held the phone at arm's length.

'Get glasses, man!' said Norva. 'So embarrassing.'

'Oh,' Pap said.

'Oh?' I asked.

'It's Ben. Ben Clarke. Katarzyna's dad,' he said.

Interesting. I looked over at Norva. She was already staring at Pap intensely.

'Go on,' urged Norva.

'He says there's something he has to show me. Seems serious, I'll go over there now.'

He stood up from the table.

So did we.

Pap paced down the hallway. He reached for his shoes.

'We're coming with you, just let me brush my teeth quickly,' said Norva.

She ran towards the bathroom.

17

85% charged.

Pap strode across the The Tri. We followed behind.

'Girls, I told you, go home,' he said. 'Finish your breakfasts. We put a lot of effort into that.'

Norva shuddered and dramatically rolled her eyes. '*We*? Please!' she muttered under her breath.

'What was that?' said Pap without turning around.

'Nothing, nothing. We just want to see where TrojKat grew up, just for a second, and then we'll go. I promise.'

Pap sighed and kept walking.

Norva smiled. She bounced a small brown bottle between her hands.

'What's that?'

'Just a little something I picked up from the bathroom.'

I narrowed my eyes at her. 'Were you even brushing your teeth?'

She leaned over to me and exhaled in my face.

Minty fresh.

'You could have just said yes, Norva.'

'Where's the fun in that?' she replied.

I needed to know more about Katarzyna's parents for our files. I therefore obtained a selection of facts from Pap in the lift.

My findings:

- Location: Corner Two. Flat 113
- Duration on the Tri: 23 years
- Ben Clarke. Katarzyna's father. 48. Black. Bald. Brawny. British-born. Parents from St. Vincent – like Pap.
- Diana Clarke – née Nowak. 45. Pale. Pretty. Precious. From Warsaw, Poland.

Other children: None. Just Katarzyna. The family used to be close, but now Katarzyna is, and I quote Pap 'acting out'. This is why she's not staying with her parents while she's on The Tri.

That's why she was so cold about them yesterday. Pap knocked on their door. He turned to face us.

'Right, you've got your information, you've seen the flat, now go,' he said in a low voice.

'But Pap,' Norva whispered. 'Just let us just peek inside! Once you go in, we'll go home.'

She turned to face me.

She grinned. She crouched at the side of the door. She motioned me to do the same.

'No – don't do that!' Pap hissed. 'Get up!'

That wasn't happening. She pulled me down next to her.

'Norva!' Pap said. He looked down at us with anger.

The door opened.

He looked up just in time.

'Ben,' he said, warmly. 'Good to see you. Everything alright?'

'Joe – thanks for coming so quickly – appreciate it,' he said. Ben ushered him into the flat. 'Come in, follow me. It's in the living room. Shut the door, yeah?'

Pap followed him into the flat. He let Norva put her hand on the doorframe.

She swung her head quickly around and up and down the hall.

She looked up at Pap and smiled. She gave him two thumbs up.

Pap shook his head, sighed. He motioned us to go away. He pushed the door.

'Go. Now!' he whispered.

The door began to close.

I looked at Norva. She stood completely still.

She stared at the door.

Her right foot twitched.

As the door was mere millimetres from closing, she twisted her foot 180 degrees.

She lifted it, and quickly slipped it between the door and its frame. The door bounced forward, slightly. She reached out to grab it, and pulled it towards her, quietly.

She didn't close it. Of course she didn't.

She looked at me with wide eyes and a wide smile.

'Sneak game strong,' she whispered.

Norva curled her finger towards me, then pointed to her ear, then to the door.

I knew what to do – I wasn't sure I wanted to do it – but I knew it was going to happen regardless.

I placed my head against the door. Through it, I could hear Ben's voice in the distance.

I could hear an argument.

My eyes met Norva's.

She nodded.

We were going in.

Norva carefully pushed the front door open. She put her fingers to my lips. I swatted them away, irritated. I didn't need her to tell me to be quiet, or to touch me.

We stepped silently into the Clarke's hallway. Norva just front of me.

We both put our backs against the wall.

I looked down the hallway. The Clarke's flat was exactly the same layout as ours, and the exact same layout as the green room.

Long hallway to the living room and kitchen. Bedrooms and a bathroom on the right.

When I looked back at Norva, she jiggled her shoulders up and down.

She was in her element.

I wasn't.

'– you're still our daughter, Kat,' a woman's voice said. Diana, I supposed. 'What do you want us to do? Nothing? You want us to feel nothing?'

'Because it *is* nothing! It's someone being stupid! Having a laugh. You and Dad – you're too over-protective. Let me go! Stop smothering me!'

'Kat, you're still young,' Ben sighed. 'We love you and want you to be safe. And this is threatening – a direct threat!'

My heart beat rapidly in my chest. I looked over at Norva.

Her mouth hung open.

I fumbled in my pocket for my phone.

```
A threat? To Katarzyna? Who did this?
Why? When?
```

'You've been so rude to us lately. You've changed, surely you know that yourself. But we still love you. Always will. You're our baby, no matter how famous you *think* you are.'

Harsh.

'Yeah, right,' she said. 'You wouldn't care if I died.'

18

'See – this right here is exactly what I mean,' said Katarzyna. 'You don't support my stardom. You want me to fail!'

'We want you to remember that this is a difficult business. It could all go away in a second – then what? What would you have? You need to remember where you came from!' Ben's voice rose 20% in volume.

Pap coughed to clear the escalating tension. 'Now,' he interjected slowly. 'This note. Where is it?'

A note!

'OK – now this is getting good!' Norva whispered loudly in my ear.

I nudged her in the ribs.

She kicked my ankle.

Movement in the living room made us focus.

'See? You see why we're worried now, Joe?' said Diana.

'It's horrible! "Welcome home baby, It's time to die, Your final resting place? It's The Tri!" Who writes that to someone? About someone?'

`A threatening note to Katarzyna!`

Norva gasped.

'That's the thing that makes it worse though, Di,' said Ben. 'If it was written, you know, by hand, that's one thing. Or if someone typed it! But this! This thing made up of newspaper letters? It's terrifying.'

'Feels like something out of an 80s movie,' added Diana.

If it was a film, I'm sure Diana would ask the director to call 'cut.' Right now.

`A threatening note to Katarzyna created from newspapers.`

I stared at Norva. Her eyes brightly shone in the shady hallway.

She made a fist. She bit it. She shook it. She smiled at me.

I nodded back at her. I knew what she meant.

A new case. A new edition for The Tri Files.

Katarzyna's laughing made us look back down the hall.

'Sounds like my lyrics,' she said.

'Laughing, Kat? Really? Tell me which part of this is funny?' Ben shouted.

'Welcome to my life,' Katarzyna said flatly. 'And welcome to your new life as parents of a popstar. Get used to it.'

'Kat – this is normal for you? You get messages like this often?' asked Pap.

Katarzyna snorted. 'Everyday, all day. 24/7. 365. My mentions are in constant shambles.'

'Your mentions?' asked Diana.

'Social media, mum,' Katarzyna snapped. 'You know? The internet? Heard of it?'

'OK, Katarzyna, that's enough – have some respect,' Pap started.

Norva winced. 'She's not going to like that, Pap.'

100% correct assumption.

'Don't you tell me anything,' Katarzyna said with a low snarl. 'Don't you tell me that's enough. You don't know my life. You know nothing about it. You know nothing about me.'

'OK, OK,' Pap protested.

I imagined him thinking he wasn't being paid enough for this drama.

He changed the subject. Quickly. 'Diana – when did

you get this letter?'

Good work, Pap. Asking the right questions. I felt a rush of pride for him. So did Norva.

'Yes Pap, keep calm, get the facts,' she whispered. 'We should recruit him y'know?'

'He would never,' I whispered back.

'It was under our door this morning. I found it at about nine. We went to bed around eleven-thirty – I didn't notice anything then. That's right, right?'

'Yeah,' said Ben. 'Nothing strange happened last night. I heard some giggling around midnight, but that Sandra next door has got herself a new man – they're always coming and going, in and out, so I paid it no mind –'

Katarzyna coughed.

'So, this morning, we called Kat –' said Diana.

'– fifteen times. Kat, you need to answer our calls!' added Ben.

'Ben. Stop. So, she came up, we showed her, we argued about what to do, then we messaged you,' said Diana. 'We want to know what we should do.'

Pap was silent.

'I think you should call the police,' he said quietly.

'No Pap – you mean call Nik and Norva,' whispered Norva.

I put my finger to my lip. Norva rolled her eyes.

'The police?' shouted Katarzyna. 'That's well unnecessary! It's not that big of a deal!'

'It is. It's a threat. You have to be safe – they need to know,' said Pap.

'The police, Joe?' said Diana.

'After what happened with Hugo?' added Ben.

The living room was silent. No words. Until Pap quietly said 'They were doing their job.'

'A terrible job,' Norva whispered in my ear.

I turned to nod, and as I did, I heard footsteps in the corridor outside.

Then, a knock at the door.

19

Norva looked at me with wide eyes. She mouthed a very rude word, not to be repeated in these files.

Her chest rose and fell quickly. She breathed loudly through her nose.

My heart raced.

We were trapped.

'We're dead,' she hissed. 'So dead – they're going to have to bury us twice.'

'I'll get it. I need to get away from you lot, even for a second,' Katarzyna said.

We heard her move towards the hallway.

She was coming.

From my calculations based on the layout of the flat, she would spot us within four seconds if we didn't do something.

Anything.

I looked up the hallway. I saw her small socked feet coming into frame.

Two seconds away.

I grabbed Norva's arm with my left hand. With my right, I reached for the handle of the nearest door I hoped was a bedroom. I hoped it wasn't looked.

It was a bedroom. It wasn't locked.

A small win.

I imagined Norva saying we were "hashtag blessed."

I slid myself – and Norva – around the door frame and quickly, quietly shut the door.

We put our backs against it and breathed deeply. Rapidly. She reached for my hand.

I grabbed it. Our damp palms clamped together.

'Hello?' Katarzyna said cautiously. She stood outside the door to the room. Her old room, by the looks of it. Incredibly neat. Pink sheets. Black seat cushion on a pine chair by a pine desk.

'Hello?' she repeated.

I looked down. The metal door handle next to my waist moved down.

The door began to open.

Norva began to wail in fear. Inaudibly. Pantomime time.

I began to pant. I looked over at Norva, gesturing to the handle with my eyes and pushed my whole body against the door.

Norva paused her act. She nodded and mirrored my movements.

From the other side, Katarzyna rattled the handle, and pushed the door harder.

'Hello?' she demanded.

'Hello?' shouted a voice from the other side of the front door.

Afua.

'Kat, why do you keep saying "hello" and not opening the door? What's the matter with you?'

Kat stopped pushing against our door and opened the front door.

'Oh, Afua! It's you! Thank goodness you're here! I just got this note – come look at it!'

I looked over at Norva. 'Hashtag blessed.' she whispered.

20

My breathing slowed. I put my ear to the door.

'What's this note?' Afua asked.

'It's a threat,' said Ben.

'What? No!' said Afua. 'Is it bad? How bad? Why didn't you call me?'

I heard the sound of Afua scrolling through her phone.

'No messages from you, Kat. Next time, just call! I'm your manager – I need to know about these things! Anything like this, you come to me!'

Footsteps approached our door. Pap.

'Thanks for showing it to me, Ben, but I've got to get back to the girls,' he said.

Norva stifled a laugh. 'We're right here,' she whispered.

'Before I go, have you considered some protection, Katarzyna? A bodyguard?'

'I'm her bodyguard,' said Afua. 'Show me the note.'

The sound of paper being passed between palms.

A gasp.

'Wow – that's rough. We should call the police!'

'Have they been called?' said Katarzyna.

I detected slight panic in her voice. 'I think you're overreacting. TrojKat means 'triangle' in Polish? The Tri – as much as it gets on my nerves – is in my blood. I can handle myself.'

'Well, I've messaged someone from the Force for advice, someone who used to live here,' said Pap. 'She'll text back shortly, I'm sure.'

That "someone" would be Katie Smyth. 25. Back Then: our Babysitter. Now: Police Officer. Always: brilliant. Mostly.

I hunched my shoulders and stretched my neck. Pushing my back against the bedroom door was exhausting.

I turned my ear back to the door.

'I'll give you a bell when I hear anything, OK?' said Pap.

'Alright, thanks Joe – appreciate this,' said Ben.

'Thanks, Joe,' said Katarzyna, her tone scornful.

The front door opened, he stepped out.

'We have to go, too,' said Afua. 'I'm here for you, Kat. We have to plan. Let's hurry it up, please!'

'Yay,' said Katarzyna, sarcastically. 'Can't wait.'

'I don't want you doing this shoot today – please Kat,'

said Diana. Her quiet voice called from the living room.

Fast footsteps.

'I'll do what I want, Mum,' said Katarzyna.

'Please, my baby, don't do it. It's not safe,' Diana's voice was louder, now.

It trembled.

Katarzyna sighed. 'It will be fine, I'm working with the best. I'll be safe.'

'But this letter?'

The sound of crumpled paper.

'We don't know who's out there – how do I know?'

'Trust me, Diana, it's a short shoot, with only trusted people – no one will be able to reach us on the roof. I would never ever let anyone hurt her,' said Afua, quietly.

'Afua, you do your best – we know. We know you love Kat,' said Ben. 'But where is Arcadia right now? Call that Jessica, tell her it's not safe here anymore – go to New York and make your video there.'

'I'll be there soon enough,' said Katarzyna.

Silence.

'As if New York's any safer than London,' said Afua. 'Safer than your own ends? Nah. I'll watch over Kat, I promise. We're going to get to get this done. We have Arcadia's money, and the best people, like Kat says.'

I looked over at Norva. She raised an eyebrow.

'Listen, we're going,' said Kat. 'I'll get this shoot planned, rehearsed and wrapped, then I'll come over.'

'You will?' said Ben.

'Yeah, there's something I want to talk to you about, actually. Once all this has died down.'

'There is?' said Afua.

'Yes,' said Katarzyna. 'I'll see you later.'

The front door closed.

21

Norva dug into her jacket pocket and pulled out her phone. She tapped out a message. I peered into her palms to see.

George.

'Why are you texting him now? We need to get out of here,' I hissed. 'That's priority number one!'

'I need updates so I'm making sure he keeps his eyes banana-peeled,' she whispered. 'This whole thing just got wild; he needs to fully scope the scene until we get up there obvs.'

'Norva –' I began.

'Sis,' she said, 'this is interesting, right?'

I nodded. It was.

'We have a case on our hands, here, yes?'

'Yes, we do,' I replied.

She squealed. I nudged her to stay quiet, but another ripple of excitement ran through me.

'OK – so we have to get started, right?'

'Right,' I said. 'But I really need to get to the computer and set it all out properly –'

She shook her head. 'Forget that for now.'

Norva looked around Katarzyna's room. She extended her arms. 'Look where we are – TrojKat's room. What a blessing. We can have a properly good rummage while we're here.'

She rubbed her hands together. 'Who knows what we'll find!'

She stepped away from the door.

'No!' I said, loudly. I slapped my hand to my mouth. 'We have to stay here!' I whispered.

'Pffft,' she replied. 'What good are we glued to the door? This investigation will officially go nowhere.'

She was right.

She walked towards the bed and sat on it. She wriggled her eyebrows. 'Sitting on a superstar's bed, what's left to be said?' she sang.

'My sister's lost her head, we're certainly dead,' I replied.

Norva stifled a laugh. 'And you think you're not creative? Lies. Right, let's case this joint.'

I cautiously stepped away from the door.

I kept one eye on it. I used one eye to look around the room. I was drawn to Katarzyna's desk.

There was a school photograph and three black wire-bound notebooks neatly stacked on top of each other on the tidy, light brown desk.

Norva reached for the frame. Two rows of small children. Nine children stood in the back row, eight sat crossed legged at the front. A small class. Royal blue cardigans, stiff grey trousers and skirts, long white socks. Shiny black shoes.

She pointed to the fine-boned brown girl with long curly hair at the front. Her face in a pinched scowl. 'Ahh, look at her – she was so cute.'

Kid Katarzyna.

I pointed to a square smiling girl. Smooth dark skin. Short twisted hair. 'Is that Afua?'

Norva peered at the photo. 'It is, ahhh! Cute!'

Norva twisted the photo towards the window. She kissed her teeth. 'Whoever took this is a disgrace to be honest, light the dark people properly – let the beauty shine!'

She returned the photo to the desk, shaking her head.

I opened the first notebook. Pages and pages of scrawled song lyrics. Thick black ink. Almost illegible.

I read some. Or tried to.

Kat's bop

My name is Kat, I live on The Tri
This is the place where dreams go to die
Every night I come home, and want to cry
Waiting for the day to say goodbye
See ya, Tri, I say goodbye
See ya, Tri, I say goodbye
See ya, Tri, I say goodbye

Norva leaned over my shoulder and mouthed the words.

'Wow, that's TrojKat?' She shook her head. 'Bit basic.'

I nodded, but in truth it sounded alright to me.

I reached for my phone. 80% battery. 11:15.

I took a photograph. Norva nodded. Her eyes were bright. I closed the notebook and reached for the one underneath.

Pages and pages of neat song lyrics. Thin blue pen. Small upper-case letters.

I read some. Easily.

Waterworks

I look at you, you don't see me (me)
We're not in the place we used to be (be)
No – as you move towards the sun (sun)

New life begins, endless fun (fun)
No – I retreat, I stay inside
But keep you forever in my mind (yes)
I'll hold on to your smirks and irks
But you can keep the waterworks.

I took a photograph.

'Deep,' said Norva. 'It's like *Cusp*.' Her eyes were closed. 'You know what that is? It's progress. That's the TrojKat I love. This is what we came for!'

'Is it now?' said a deep voice in the doorway.

Ben.

Diana stood behind him.

I dropped my phone.

22

'What *the hell* are you doing here?' shouted Diana. 'Why are you in our house?'

Ben reached into his pocket for his phone. 'These are Joe's girls – wait until he finds out about this.'

I stared at them. I began to shake. I blinked.

I opened my mouth to speak, but no sounds emerged.

I'm not 100% certain what words would have come out, anyway.

Ben began to type a message. To Pap, I presumed.

I looked over at Norva. She quickly glanced at me.

'Thank god you're here!' Norva shouted. She rushed towards Ben and Diana. She embraced them. An arm each. She held onto them tightly.

In the bemusement, I leant over and reached for my phone, and put it back in my pocket.

Norva started sobbing.

'We got stuck – we didn't know how to get out! The door – we couldn't open it,' she cried. 'My sister –' she looked over at me, smiled briefly, before reverting to her wailing – 'my sister tried to get us out, but we were so scared – so scared of what you would say!'

Diana looked at me. I nodded.

'Yes. I was scared,' I said.

Norva turned her head and narrowed her eyes at me.

'Yes, sorry – I was terrified. Terrified!'

I *was* scared – but dramatic expression is just not my strength.

'We shouldn't have been here,' Norva said.

'No, you absolutely shouldn't be – why are you?' said Ben.

'That a good question,' said Norva.

It was.

'You see – we're both huge fans of TrojKat, aren't we, Nik?'

'Huge,' I lied.

'And when we met her yesterday, she didn't seem to be in a good mood – at all.'

'Sounds about right,' sighed Ben.

'She also told me about the time I vomited in her hair when I was a baby,' Norva sobbed. 'I was gutted.'

'She's still going on about that?' said Diana quietly. She

folded her arms.

'So when Pap said he was coming over here, we wanted to leave her a secret present.'

We did?

'You did?' said Ben.

'Yes,' Norva and I said in unison.

Norva reached into her pocket. She pulled out the small brown bottle from the bathroom.

'This is really great shampoo,' she said. 'Shea butter and almond oil. We thought she would like it!' Norva burst into tears. 'Please don't tell Pap! W-w-we just wanted to make it up to her! We were just trying to make her happy.' Norva gasped for air between words, like a fish fresh out of water.

Ben sighed. He put his phone back into his pocket.

'I understand that feeling,' he said.

23

Norva gulped down her water. Her hands trembled around the glass.

An Oscar-worthy performance. Best Actress in a Fumbled Sneak-In.

'Th-thanks Ben,' she said. She stood by their kitchen counter. 'And thank you both for not telling Pap – we appreciate it.'

I nodded. 'It's really good of you.' It was.

I looked at Norva, but she wasn't looking back at me.

I followed her eyes.

She was looking at a folded piece of paper on the counter. It lay between two clearly-used mugs and a jar of instant coffee.

Her fingers inched towards it.

'So how much of our conversation did you hear? Do you know why your Dad was here?' Ben said. He sat at his table. Diana in the chair next to him. He turned to look at Norva.

Norva snatched her encroaching hand away and shook her head. 'No – Pap doesn't chat about anyone else's business. He's the manager here, it would be a bad look.'

She stared at me.

She pointed to the slip of paper. She wriggled her fingers towards it and narrowed her eyes.

'Yes, it would be very unprofessional,' I said.

'Excellent' Ben said with a chuckle. 'He's a good man, it was terrible what happened to him this summer.'

I tensed at the mention of summer.

I thought of the heat, the smell, the pain.

I remembered the deep worry. I remembered Hugo.

'Yes,' I said. 'He is.'

For a moment I didn't know if I was talking about Pap or Hugo.

I quickly realised I was talking about both.

I cleared my throat.

'Why was he here? Can you tell us?' I said.

Diana sat up straight and reached for Ben's hand. He held it gently in his lap.

'We worry about our daughter – just like your Dad worries about you both, I'm sure,' said Diana.

I shrugged. 'I suppose. What are you so worried about?' I asked.

'Well, she's getting very successful –'

The sound of coffee cups clinking on the counter.

'But the new Arcadia deal is amazing, isn't it?' I said, louder. I coughed.

I looked at Norva. I looked at the kitchen counter.

The piece of paper was gone.

Ben snorted. 'It's all right.'

Diana squeezed Ben's hand.

'No – it is great. It's wonderful. It gets her out of here; she doesn't like it much,' said Diana.

We knew. We could tell.

Ben looked out of the window. 'She needs to remember where she came from and have some respect, Di. I worry she's making enemies out there – enemies close to home.'

'Enemies?' Norva asked.

Diana squeezed Ben's hand. Tighter this time. 'It's good that she has her friends around her – Afua and Simon – that boy she's been seeing –'

I looked at Norva. She was already looking at me.

'– we don't know even know who he is!' said Ben. 'We used to know everyone!' He threw his hands up in frustration. 'She barely talk to us anymore, and when she does, she's rude.'

This was a fact. Evidence? Her consistent behaviour since we met.

'Yeah,' Diana said softly. 'I don't blame her. She wants

to get out of this place. She is 23, Ben. Kids grow up – they change.'

'I know, – but I miss her.' Ben shook his head. He sighed. 'I just don't think this whole moving to New York thing is going to end well.'

We sat in a brief silence.

Oooooh Oooooh

Until Norva's phone broke it.

She placed her glass of water on the counter. 'Thank you *so* much for everything,' she said. 'But we have to go.'

24

'Was that from Pap?' I craned my neck to look at Norva's phone.

The lift in Corner One approached the 22nd floor. Heading home.

'Nah, George.'

'And?'

'And what?'

'And what did he say?!'

'Oh yeah… no useful intel yet. He's trapped. His Aunt Geeta is over – her new dude's done a runner and his mum's gone out. He's furious and trying to hurry her but, as he says, "family first".'

'How frustrating for him,' I said.

'For him? What about us? But yeah, I told him to just bounce, leave her, get up there.' Norva chuckled. 'Aunty G getting ghosted again. On Halloween? How tragically on-brand for her.'

'That's not very nice.'

'Honestly, who cares about be being *nice* right now? We've got bigger fish to fry!'

She reached into her pocket and gently pulled out a piece of paper. 'I have the note!' she sung. 'Beautiful distraction back there, Nik' she said. 'Nicely done.'

The lift shuddered to a halt.

She placed the note back in her pocket.

'Thanks. I wish it wasn't in your pocket, though, it's so contaminated. There's so much potential evidence on it − hair, saliva, fingerprints.' I sighed

'Yeah, true,' said Norva. 'But it was doing the rounds like pass-the-parcel down there from the sound of it. Everyone had their filthy mitts on it at one point.'

'True,' I said. 'Pap and Afua definitely touched it − and of course Katarzyna and her parents.'

'Better for us have it then.'

'Yes.'

'Better for it be in my pocket then at their house, right?'

'Yes, I agree.'

Better for it to be here than next to cups of Rosta coffee, innit?'

'Alright − I said yes didn't I!'

'Relax – jeez. I was just saying!'

'You're always saying.'

Norva laughed. 'You're funny, always so snappy. Like a little bald black piranha.' She gnashed her teeth at me twice.

I rolled my eyes.

The lift opened. We walked down the corridor to our flat.

She put her key in our front door.

Pap instantly appeared in the hallway.

'Where have you been? You've just got back here? Your breakfast is freezing,' he sighed.

I looked at my phone. 12:46. 78% battery.

'Yeah, sorry Pap – we ran into George. He's well excited for the shoot, isn't he Nik?'

I looked at Norva, and then at Pap.

'Yes.' I looked at the floor.

I felt a very slight pang in the pit of my stomach.

It was increasingly getting easier to lie to Pap.

Norva had no such concerns.

She closed the door to our bedroom.

'He'll believe anything I swear,' she chuckled. 'Gullible Pap.'

'Don't, Norva. That's not nice.'

She paused for a moment. 'Yeah, you're right, it's not

– but it's totally necessary. Think of it like this: these little lies are like tiny nails in our toolbox of scammery. Small but essential.

Now –' she slapped our monitor '– get the computer on. Let's go. While we wait for George, you can get the files together.'

I sat down at our desk and shook the mouse to wake our computer.

I charged my phone.

Norva opened the doors to her wardrobe. She stroked her costume. 'I can't wait to wear you later,' she said.

I sighed.

'Are you going to tell me what it is?'

'Oh, you care now do you?' she said. 'Nope. It will be unveiled at the right time.'

She stepped out from behind her wardrobe doors.

'The document ready yet?'

The black cursor blinked on the white screen.

I nodded.

Norva clapped her hands together.

25

'I'll start,' I said. 'With a fact. Katarzyna's parents received a note. A death threat against her.'

'That she did,' said Norva.

```
Item of interest: Note
Content: Death Threat to TrojKat
Received by: Ben and Diana Clarke
```

Norva reached into her pocket. She placed the note on the desk. She smoothed it out with her palms. She peered over my shoulder.

We looked at it together.

Welcome HOme, Baby
IT's time to DiE
your FiNaL resTiNg pLace?
It's THE TRI!

The W of Welcome looked familiar. I leaned closer to look.

'This is super messed up. I know she's in diva mode right now – even I can imagine how annoying that would be on a full-time basis – but this? This is a lot. This is TrojKat for crying out loud! Who would hurt her?'

'Wait, wait, Norva – let's get more facts down first, before we get to suspects. There's a process. The note was delivered under their door.'

```
Location: 2/113
```

Norva nodded. 'Last night, between, between,' she drummed her finger against her lip. 'What time was it again?'

'Between eleven-thirty and nine am this morning, Norva. That's what Ben said.'

```
Delivery window: 30/10 23:30 - 31/10
09:00
```

'That window is so wide open, we'll catch a chill. We have to narrow that down.'

'Absolutely,' I said. I thought for a moment. 'Wait – Ben said something about hearing someone –'

'– Sandra,' said Norva with certainty.

'How do you remember that, but not the time?'

She shrugged. 'I'm good with names.'

I continued. 'Ben said he may have heard Sandra and her boyfriend around midnight, didn't he?'

'Yep – we gotta find Sandy and her man, then! An action!'

'Do you know her? I don't recall any Sandra living in Corner Two – not by name at least.'

'Nope. But I'd like to meet her. She might have been the noise they heard – or she might have seen something herself.'

```
Delivery window: 30/10 23:30 - 31/10
09:00. Possibly midnight?
To do: Locate Sandra
```

'What else do we know?' I asked. 'For certain.'

Norva walked to the window and peered out. She put her left hand on the glass, her right on the telescope.

'We know that this note is made from letters from newspapers, don't we?' she said, her back to me.

'Yes,'

'And who did we see buying loads of newspapers, in Better Buy last night?'

I sat up straight in the chair.

'James Paul Dean.' I said. 'He bought five.'

I jumped up and plunged my hand into my jeans pocket. I had the evidence. 'I have the receipt! Look – the newspapers are all listed. The Daily Flash, The Signal, The Paladin, This Moment, The New York Witness –'

'Didn't Sissy say something about that New York one last night?'

'She did!' I said. 'She said it was the only copy she had. And look – that first "W" on the letter is a style match. I knew I recognised it!'

'Brilliant. See, I told you – always worth keeping receipts,' said Norva smugly. 'Make James Paul Dean an official suspect.'

I sat down. Norva continued.

'Old News bought the newspapers and put that letter together – my stomach is saying yes – let's go find him and call him out,' said Norva.

I leaned back in my chair.

'Wait, Norva – we also saw James and Katarzyna kissing last night.'

'I know. We did.'

'And earlier, Diana said that Katarzyna was seeing someone she'd never introduced them too. If that's him –

and I think we can sensibly deduce it is – then that means he's unlikely to have done it, right? Why would you send a hate letter to someone you love?'

26

'Maybe he's faking it?' said Norva. 'What if it's a scam, and he's only pretending to be into her?'

'But what would James want from Katarzyna?'

Norva snorted. 'Come on now Nik – TrojKat is hot, she's famous, she's just signed a multi-million pound deal and everything that comes with it – mostly jealousy and drama!'

I drummed my fingers against my lips. A wave of doubt washed over me.

'I'm not so sure about this, Norva. Say they are together – surely there would be easier ways to threaten her, if that was his intention. Why send a letter to her parents' flat – when he knows she's not even staying there?'

'Good point, good point,' said Norva. 'And why send a letter made from papers, when you can just slide hate directly into people's DMs?'

'What?'

'You can just message bile directly to the person on the internet, that's nice and easy to do if that's your energy. This super old school letter reeks of effort and is an attention seek. Why?'

I thought for a moment.

'Perhaps someone who saw him with the newspapers is framing him?' I said.

Norva spun away from the window and turned to face me. 'I just got epic tingles at that suggestion! That's a real possibility. The intrigue, yes! What else?'

'Well, this letter has definitely come from James Paul Dean's newspapers, and therefore someone directly connected to the shoot.'

'Agree, and Katarzyna was trying to keep this shoot on the hush hush' said Norva.

'She didn't want to draw that much attention to herself – she didn't want to go to Bermuda's.'

'Total agreement' said Norva. 'That confirms it – so who could it be?'

'So, who knew about the video shoot?'

'Well,' said Norva. 'You and me knew. And Pap.'

I looked at Norva. 'It certainly wasn't me. I don't have any motive – and I'm 98% certain it wasn't you. We watched TV and went to bed.'

Norva clutched her hands to her chest. 'You have such

faith in me, I love you.' She narrowed her eyes. 'Where's that 2% doubt coming from though?'

I smiled. 'I trust no one,' I said. 'But you were also asleep at the time of delivery – and you've been trying to make friends with Katarzyna and not deepen the divide. I don't see you doing it. To quote you, "that's not your energy."'

'Exactly, it's not very much. Rule. Us. Out.' Norva slapped the desk between words. 'I don't think you did it either.'

'Done,' I said.

'And Pap – he helped her get the flat. He has zero motive, and absolutely no reason to bring Police attention to himself again,' said Norva.

I agreed. 'What about George?'

Norva stood up straight. 'Now, now – my boy would never.' She shook her head. 'Nope.'

'He went home early last night.' I paused. 'Are we certain he was where he said he was?' I said.

Norva was quiet.

'And this morning, he's not at the shoot… the shoot he's been excited about for months? Is he feeling too guilty to go?'

'Behave,' said Norva.

'Since he's your best friend, maybe he made the note as

way of getting you on the shoot?'

'Now that would be a power move for the ages,' laughed Norva. 'However — and I say this with love — George doesn't have the range for that kind of duplicity. Not his style.' Norva shook her head. 'Nope. He wouldn't be this vintage about it either. Imagine if he did — our detective duo would become a trio before you could even blink, I swear.'

'I could be open to further discussion on his participation further at a later date, Norva, but for now I still have to add him to the list — until we have evidence to the contrary.'

'Fine,' said Norva. 'He's going to be mad at you for that though.'

27

'Right, real suspects now,' said Norva. 'What about Afua? 'We know her and Katarzyna have been friends for donkeys, Ben and Diana said she basically used to live there.'

I nodded. 'We saw her in their school photograph, which corroborates that.' I paused, thinking back to the photograph.

'What if Afua sent that note to make Katarzyna feel unsafe?' I wondered.

'Why?' added Norva

'So she could save the day and prove herself to be a great manager – therefore securing her place in Katarzyna's life?' I offered.

'That's actually really strong,' said Norva. 'Superglue strong. Write it down. It would totally not be my way of doing things though.'

'What do you mean?'

'Look, if I was a celebrity – which I totally could be one

day – and someone was threatening me? Where I live? I'd be on the first plane out of here. See ya, suckers – I'm out. Gone.'

'You have a point. It wouldn't be the most effective way to keep someone on side,' I said. 'And Afua genuinely didn't seem to know about the note when they talked in the hallway.'

Norva nodded. 'She didn't seem to – but she wouldn't give it away if she was the one who sent it, would she?'

'Point taken. Okay, let's find out what Afua's plans are – if Katarzyna is going to leave London, is she going too?'

'Good idea. Note that all down, please.'

'I am,' I sighed. 'You don't need to tell me.'

'Snapping again, sis. Relax. Now Simon. What about Simon – is he feeling threatened by Kat leaving? If so – why?' Norva stroked her chin.

'Ben and Diana said that Simon also spent a lot of time at their house, and they're close too. We need to know how close they are.'

'That we do,' said Norva. 'Also, when did they become friends? I didn't spot him in the school photo.'

'I think they met at sixth form college,' I said. 'Afua said something about your infamous puking incident happening before "his time."'

Norva sighed. 'They just won't let me move on from

that will they?' I shook my head. 'Anyway, back to Simon – what else do we know about him?'

'He used to work in news – when did he change jobs?'

Norva shrugged.

'This is where George may actually be useful for once,' I said.

'Totally,' said Norva. 'We need him up there with them, sending intel down to us.'

'Yes,'

Norva tapped out a message on her phone. 'I'm seeing if he's there yet.'

'Great,' I said. 'Now Hester. What are the facts?'

'We know there was scorching hot tension between her and Three Names in Bermuda's last night. She touched his arm and he sent the drinks flying!'

'Yes, that's right – we need to understand that interaction.'

'I think I have an idea,' said Norva, stroking her chin. 'We can tell they have history, and there's a connection.'

'She messaged him and him only when she arrived last night,' I said. 'If it was strictly business, I would have expected her to message Afua, since she's in charge – or at least I think she is.'

'Exactly. So, what about this? James – I can't be bothered to keep saying all of his names, life's too short –

James and Hester are together.'

'OK,' I said. 'Feasible.'

'James has been having a secret affair with Katarzyna. Hester's found out, and put the note together using James' papers, threatening Katarzyna while also getting revenge on him. Two outcomes, one action.'

28

'That's solid,' I said. 'Plausible.'

'I know,' said Norva. 'I'm a professional. Now we need to know what time they all bounced from Bermuda's – understand what kind of time they hand on their hands.

'Well, we saw The Kissing occur at approximately 21:35. So after that?'

'Excellent,' said Norva. She looked out of our window. 'Hmmm…'

'…hmmm what?'

'Nah, nah, never mind. It's a real reach.'

I turned in my chair to look at her.

'No go on – what are you thinking?'

'I've just got this vibe, this feeling –'

'Out with it, Norva,'

'What if the note was made by someone closer to Chez Clarke?'

'Who?'

'Ben and Diana?'

'Her own parents?' I stroked my chin. 'Controversial. List your reasons.'

Norva jumped over to her bed. 'OK, so – we definitely know Katarzyna and her parents have been arguing.'

She lay down.

'Yes, they had to call her fifteen times before she visited this morning,'

'Right. And Ben was well vexed with her.'

I thought back to our conversation with him, and the ones we overheard.

I nodded. 'He did say she was making enemies close to home.'

'Exactly – you can't get closer to home than your own house. Can you? Can you now?'

You couldn't.

'But does it make sense to scare your own daughter like that?' I asked. 'It seems like an incredibly cruel thing to do. How would they have got those newspapers? The one copy of The New York Witness?'

Norva shrugged. 'I don't know. All right, it's not very likely. I just thought Ben wanted to scare her into behaving better – to check herself, before she wrecks herself?'

'That's extremely extreme. Pap would never do that to me. He might do that to you, though, Norva.'

'Funny. But desperate times call for desperate measures. Ben did say he had a feeling this whole thing wasn't going to end well.'

'He did. But the evidence with the newspapers rules them out,' I said. 'They didn't have the paper – it wasn't them'

'OK, fine,' said Norva. 'I did say it was a reach.'

I stretched and wriggled my fingers. I had a thought.

'How's this for close to home, Norva – what if Katarzyna created the note herself?'

I knew from experience that this was not an impossible scenario.

Norva rose zombie-like from the bed.

'Did you just see that? I'm definitely breaking out that move later.' She laughed. 'Now back on topic – that's a very interesting idea indeed.' She stroked her chin. 'Why would she do that?'

'Attention? She did get much more upset when Afua arrived. To get something? To frame someone?'

'Ooh, yeah, maybe!'

'Remember when delivered her shopping, we overheard her?' I said.

'Yes! She said,' Norva mimicked her voice, 'We have a plan, we need to stick to it!'

'Was the note the plan? Was the other person backing out?'

'Ooh my gosh,' Norva whispered. 'She was working with someone? Sick!'

'But who?'

Ooooooh Oooooh

Norva's phone. She reached for it and stood up straight.

'OK, George is in the green room. I repeat. George is in the green room.'

She walked over to the desk.

'Have you told him about the note, yet?'

She leaned over and took a photograph.

'You read my mind.'

Oooooh Oooooh

Norva laughed.

'What?'

'He just replied with a face of screaming emojis.'

Ring! Ring!

George.

Norva answered the phone. She put it on loudspeaker.

'Oh my days – I had to call you.' George whispered.

'I'm outside the flat, hence the low tone. That message? Is it legit – or are NSquared having an arts and crafts moment?'

'Nope,' said Norva. 'We can't take the credit for this one. It's really real. George – we've had the wildest morning, snuck into Katarzyna's parents place –'

'You didn't!'

'– got captured by her parents –'

'Why are you like this? I –'

'We've just been going through all the suspects.'

'I bet!' said George. He laughed. 'Nik's got the documents all straight already right? That's so her. I better not be on that list.'

'I can hear you George,' I said. 'And you are.'

George coughed. 'Norva – what have I told you? You've gotta let people know when they're on speaker – that's the rules. I don't make them,' he said sternly. His voice softened. 'Alright, Nik? You good? I didn't send that letter, behave. I love TrojKat, I'm not about that life.'

'Hmmm,' I said.

In the distance, another voice.

'George – you in or out? It's after one, you've just got here and now you're taking calls? We don't have time for anymore family drama. I've had enough of that noise already today'

'Sorry sorry sorry,' George replied. 'Just coming, Afua.'

A door slammed.

'Listen, I gotta roll, I –'

'George, no!' Norva interrupted 'You need to get us up there – we need access. Now!' This is more than a shoot – it's a full on case'

'Alright alright. Come now – I'll figure something out while on your way. I hope.'

Item of interest: Note

Content: Death Threat to TrojKat made from newspaper letters

Received by: Ben and Diana Clarke

Motive: TBC

Location: 2/113

Delivery window: 30/10 23:30 – 31/10 09:00 Possibly midnight?

To do: Find out when everyone left Bermuda's

To do: Locate Sandra (Ben and Diana's neighbour)

Suspect	Relationship to Trojkat	Motive
James Paul Dean (JPD – aka Old News)	* Stunt coordinator on shoot * KC's secret boyfriend?	Jealousy? Money? Drama?
George Shah (GS)	* Fan * Working with SB on the shoot	Get Norva onto the shoot?
Afua Martey (AM)	* Best friend * Manager (for now)	Wants to stay in KC's life?
Simon Brook (SB)	* Works on sound * Friends with AM and KC * Used to work in News	Wants to stay in KC's life?

Movements	Questions
* 30/11 18:30 Better Buy - 5x Newspapers 3x Beast Bites * 30/11 19:32 Bermuda's - Tense conversation with Hester * 30/11 21:47 Kissing KC outside Bermuda's	* What is your relationship with HB? * What is your relationship with KC?
* 30/11 19:45 Went to bed early to prepare * 31/11 13:01 Arrives late to shoot for personal reasons	* Did Aunt Geeta really come over?
* 30/11 19:30 Bermuda's	* What are her plans once KC moves to NYC? * How close are they since KC signed with Arcadia?
* 30/11 19:30 Bermuda's	* How close are they since KC signed with Arcadia?

Suspect	Relationship to Trojkat	Motive
Hester Bos (HB)	* Director on the shoot	Was in relationship with JPD? Jealous of KC?
Katarzyna Clarke (KC – aka TrojKat)	* Is TrojKat! The star of the show	Attention? Framing someone?

Movements	Questions
* 30/11 19:32 Bermuda's – Tense conversation with JPD	* What is the status of her relationship to JPD?
* 30/11 18:50 Heated conversation out side 2/223 * 30/11 21:47 Kissing JPD outside Bermuda's	* Who was she on the phone to? * What was the plan that needs sticking to? * If she created the note, was she working with someone else? * Is she definitely moving to NYC? * What is she going to tell her parents?

29

'Can we rely on George to get us in?'

'Yep,' said Norva. 'We can.'

I pushed the button for the lift. 'So, what are we going to do, just knock on the door and walk in?'

'Pretty much,'

'Pretty much, Norva? That's the plan?'

We stepped into the lift. I pressed the button to take us to the ground floor.

'Yeah – don't worry about it,'

I was worried.

The lift quickly came to stop. Floor 21. One floor below ours.

The doors opened.

In stepped Nina Shah. 37. Short, small body, long, inky-black hair. George's mother. Behind her, an almost identical woman. Only slightly taller. And much more morose. She sniffed. She dabbed at her eyes.

Aunt Geeta.

'Hi girls,' said Nina. 'How are you?'

I looked over at Norva. She shrugged and nodded. Her gesture said 'Go ahead – ask them about George.'

'We're good, thanks,' I replied. 'How are you? Busy morning?'

Aunt Geeta sniffed loudly.

Nina looked at me. She rolled her eyes.

'You could say that. Went out for a run this morning, then ran some errands. Got stuck on the Tube, and then came back to find Geeta with George.'

Aunt Geeta wailed.

'I'm having a bad day,' Geeta said. A tear rolled down her face. 'A really bad one.'

I felt sorry for her. So I told her.

'I'm sorry to hear that.'

'She shrugged. 'It is what it is.'

'How's George?' said Norva. 'We haven't heard from him all day.'

Nina shook her head. 'He was in a bit of mood when I left him. He had to stay with Geeta until I got back – you know, family first.'

I nodded.

Nina sighed, 'So he was late to his shoot – the one he's been talking about non-stop for months.' Nina laughed. 'He was in bed by eight last night to prepare – can you believe it? My George? Sleeping soundly and everything.'

Norva looked at me. 'I definitely believe it,' she said. 'Do you, Nik?'

I nodded. 'I do.'

***

'Told you!' said Norva. 'I told you it wasn't George!'

'I know you did – and to be quite honest – he was only on the suspect list for completeness.'

Norva chuckled.

We were in another lift. Corner Three, this time. The green room beckoned.

I looked at my phone. Our ETA? Approximately 90 seconds.

90% charge.

'We had to rule him out – and I'm glad we have. He is officially removed from the investigation. His alibi has now been corroborated.'

'"Corroborated", you know. Your formalities crack me up, I love it.'

'I'm glad you do. I can't say I love your lack of plan, however,' I said. 'We're going to be there in a moment.'

The lift stopped.

'See? We're here.'

Norva nodded. 'I know.'

'What are we going to say to all of these people – people who don't want us around?'

The lift doors opened.

'Norva – say something! The plan?'

'They'll be pleased to see us.'

'Norva – what are you talking about!'

She walked towards the door of Flat 223.

She knocked on the door. Loudly.

'Norva, please!' I begged.

It opened. A sliver. George.

Voices arguing behind him.

I definitely didn't want to go in there.

Norva nodded at George. He nodded back.

'Keys,' he whispered.

Keys? I was confused.

Norva nodded.

She wasn't.

'Nice one,' she said. 'Proud of you, G.'

George smiled. He opened the door wider. 'Yo, NSquared! Come in, come in!' He said with a smile. He shouted into the hallway. 'They're here! I reckon they can sort this out.'

I glared at Norva and George through narrowed eyes.

Norva put her hand on my shoulder. 'Go with it,' she said.

I didn't want to.

We stepped into the flat. The snake pit.

My gut ached with dread.

I walked slowly down the hallway behind Norva and George.

My heart rate began to rise.

I gulped. My mouth dry.

I did not like these people. At all.

They were not to be trusted.

Not a single one of them.

30

The crew didn't acknowledge our presence.

Of course they didn't.

Not that I expected them to, I knew what kind of people they were.

Rude ones.

Potentially dangerous ones.

On second thoughts, I was pleased to be ignored. I stood close to Norva and George.

Katarzyna sat alone on the small black sofa. The living room was now filled with equipment. Tall lights, large speakers, a small camera.

She stared at her phone.

She flicked her thumb rhythmically at her screen and laughed.

The rest of her crew sat on chairs around the table. Planning.

Afua, Simon and the woman with the black bob and red lips – Hester – looked intently at pieces of paper, while James Paul Dean talked and pointed.

'To recap. Kat's standing at the edge. Her back to camera. Simon – cue the music.'

Simon nodded.

'On the line "When every day you rise?" Kat is looking back at you, Hester.'

Hester crossed her arms. She sighed.

'Next line,' said James Paul Dean. 'Do you watch me fall? Kat falls straight down, back to camera.'

On the piece of paper, he drew a long line to the bottom edge of the paper. He looked up and pointed at Hester.

'Hester – you're on her with your camera, you're leaning over the edge. Camera straight down.'

Hester shook her head. She sighed deeply through her nose. She stared out of the window.

'Then she walks backwards up the side of the building. Stunt over. Simple.'

'Sounds amazing,' said Afua. 'Really, James, I think that will look stunning.'

'Amazing?' said Hester. 'Stunning, really? Am I the director here or are you, James?'

James shuffled the papers on the table. 'I need to be across this scene, I'm here for the stunt, remember?'

'Your stunt is pointless – if you can't see her face, why do it? Where is the emotion? Where is its reasoning? It lacks context.'

'It's better this way,' said James.

Hester snorted. 'It's not.'

'It's fine,' said Afua.

'It's not fine at all, Afua,' said Hester.

Silence.

Katarzyna chuckled into her phone.

100% disinterest.

Hester threw up her hands.

'This shoot is a mess! How could you lose the keys to the location, Afua? I haven't even been to the roof yet!'

George looked us. Norva smiled at him.

'My boy,' she mouthed. She slapped her chest twice with pride.

'We haven't lost them – they're just... misplaced,' said Afua.

'What's the difference? Hester shouted.

There was none. Afua looked at the floor.

'Why don't you just call the building manager if you've lost the keys?' snapped Hester. 'Just get another set?'

Katarzyna quickly looked up from her phone and her eyes met Afua's. Katarzyna shook her head. Afua nodded.

Pap's presence was not wanted here.

'Er, no,' said Afua. 'He's busy.'

'A busybody,' said Katarzyna.

My body temperature rose three degrees. My hands balled into a fist.

Your parents called him this morning. My parent was very much not interested in being part of your drama.

I think I hated her. Kat. Katarzyna. TrojKat. Whatever. All iterations equalled irritation.

She was so rude. So rude.

George coughed.

'Yeah, so about these keys, Nik and Norva will know how to get a new set. That's why I called them.'

'Who are these children?' asked Hester, she stared at James.

'Building manager's daughters. George's friends,' said Simon.

Hester rolled her eyes. 'Is this a creche? Am I directing a kindergarten or a music video? James, what is this?'

Afua turned in her chair. 'Could you get us a key? To the roof? Would you do that?'

Katarzyna looked up from her phone. She sighed. 'Of course they can't, Afua. Why are you even asking? It's too much for them, definitely too scary for Norva. You want her vomming with nerves all over the place? Katarzyna shuddered. She leaned over and reached into her bag. She rubbed her hand sanitizer all over her hands while she stared at Norva. 'I did promise your Dad I'll keep this place tidy, didn't I?' She smiled. 'Get out.'

Norva sighed deeply.

'Look, Katarzyna,' said Norva. 'I'm not that baby anymore, I've grown up. I'll show you. I'll get those keys.'

31

George, Norva and I stood outside the green room.

The voices in the living room continued to argue behind us. The music of the moment.

'Yes, George,' whispered Norva. 'Beautifully done. Beautifully done!' She kissed her fingers. 'Delicious.'

She put her hand out. 'Now give me the key. We'll take it, we'll walk around for ten or so minutes, make it seem legit – then return to the scene as heroes.'

George grinned. He patted down his pockets.

A wave of panic swept across his face.

'It's not here,' he said. 'It's not here!' He said, louder. 'I had it – I did!'

'So you've lost the 'lost' keys?' I said.

George nodded. 'I think so, yeah?'

I shook my head.

'I'm sorry NSquared – it was right here! Guess my spy skills aren't fully up to scratch, after all.'

'Well you call them 'spy skills' for a start,' I said. 'That's your first mistake.'

Norva rolled her eyes. 'George – do you know how much more difficult you've just made this?'

**

Norva opened our front door at 13:35.

'Pap?' Norva shouted as the door opened. 'You home?'

'Yeah, Norv – on the sofa,' he shouted back down the hallway.

Norva slumped against the wall.

'Eurgh,' said Norva. 'Why couldn't he actually be at Jane's when we needed him to be? Make this easy for us?' She looked down the corridor. 'We need The Bunch.'

The Bunch. Pap's spare keys.

'You know what to do,' she said.

It wasn't a question. It was a request.

Norva walked slowly down the hall, her head down.

I followed behind her.

'Pap,' she said. She kneeled in front of him on the sofa. 'I feel terrible. I'm so embarrassed about Kat and the vomiting.' Her voice wavered. She looked at Pap. 'I wanted to impress her so much. It's been bothering me all night and all day!'

Norva burst into tears. Pap leaned forward quickly to comfort her and sat on the floor to embrace her.

'Oh, love, I know, I know,' he said. He smoothed Norva's braids. He put his face against her head. 'It's OK.'

The coast was clear. I quickly paced into the kitchen on my tip toes. I slowly opened the kitchen drawer. The keys that usually sat on top weren't there. I'd have to go in.

'She spoke to me like I'm an idiot, like I'm worthless!' wailed Norva.

Pap drew her closer.

'I know,' said Pap. 'And I'm sorry about that. Fame has gone to her head.'

I delicately picked up a letter – HMRC. I slowly picked up some screwed-up tissues – disgusting. I picked up a small screwdriver. I saw them. The keys were in the very back of the drawer. Great.

'I'm not worthless, am I Pap?' Norva sobbed.

I reached my arm into the drawer. I blindly felt for the keys. They jangled. I had them.

'Absolutely not,' said Pap, soothingly. 'Never say that about yourself.'

Norva wailed.

This was it. My moment.

I pulled the keys out. I ran to the cupboard, grabbed a

glass and filled it with water. I coughed.

Norva pulled away from Pap's hug.

'So yeah,' she said, wiping her eyes. 'She made me feel well bad.' She looked at me.

I nodded. Norva stood up. She wiped her eyes.

'I'm going to go for a walk, get some fresh air, think about what I've done.'

Pap narrowed his eyes.

We paced quickly down the hall and shut the door behind us.

I stared at her as we waited for the lift.

'Bit much, Norva?'

'What? Kat did make me feel horrible. Where was the lie?'

32

Pap's Office.

Ground floor of Corner One.

Norva unlocked the door, shutting it quietly behind her. I didn't turn Pap's desk light on. We didn't need the attention. I switched on the torch on my phone.

'Shine that on the floor, now!' She whispered. 'And get down.'

I crouched. Norva spread The Bunch on the floor. 'Right, which one is for the security box?' She pointed to the metal case on the wall. 'I don't know why he locks it. If he locks the main door, what's the point?'

'For safety, Norva?'

'Alright, alright – it just seems so extra. Locks on lockdown.' I shook my head. 'It's that one there.' I pointed to a small silver key.

'Sure? How can you tell?' She said.

'Well, the number on it is 31801, I wouldn't forget that,' I laughed.

'What's so funny?'

'So?'

'You don't think that's a cool coincidence?'

'Erm, I don't even get it.'

I sighed. 'We live on The Tri – and it has three tower blocks. That's the three.'

'Okay...'

'The interior angles of any triangle add up to one hundred and eighty.'

'Right…?'

'And we live in Corner One. 3. 180. 1?' I said.

'You're so offbeat,' she said with a smile.

We stood up, she tried the key, and it worked. She slapped me on the back.

'Eurgh, what a time-saving queen – now shine your light up here.'

I did. The light reflected on at least 200 sets of keys.

'Gah,' she said. 'This is going to take forever.'

'It's not – they're all in order, just give me a second. I –'

As I reached for the keys, Pap's office door handle rattled.

'Get down!' hissed Norva. 'Get under the desk and cut your light!'

The handle rattled for a second time.

We crouched under the desk in the dark.

Heart pumping. Mind racing.

The door opened.

I reached for Norva's hand with my free one. She squeezed it back immediately.

'Oh, it's open – great,' said a now-familiar male voice.

James Paul Dean.

'No talking, James, just looking.' said Hester. 'We're losing light and we can't rely on infants.'

Norva squeezed my hand.

Hester and James walked to the security box.

James sighed. 'We're not going to figure this out, Hester. Let's go. Let's give those girls a chance – we've got no option.'

'Fine,' said Hester. 'But since we have a moment alone, James –'

Silence, then the sound of kissing.

Norva looked at me.

'No, Hester, stop. Stop! I told you! I'm not interested anymore. Don't do this.'

'You're not interested? I mostly took this job to be close to you again! Why else would I be here?'

'The money? The experience? The creativity?'

'The creativity, that is true,' said Hester with a sigh. 'Because you, James, are a complete waste of time.' She walked to the door.

'Hester —' James replied. He followed behind her.

I counted to nine in my head. 'I think we can get up now,' I whispered to Norva. She tried to nod, and she did. Straight into my forehead.

'Owww!' I wailed.

Norva's hand flew to my mouth. 'Shhhh, I'm sorry, I'm sorry!'

We stood up. I turned on my phone's torch with one hand and touched my head gingerly with the other.

I shone the torch on Norva. She grinned wildly.

'Hester and James then?' She squealed. 'We knew it!'

I nodded.

'Right,' she said, 'Now let's grab those keys and get back up there.'

33

Corner Three. In the lift. The green room beckoned.

'Were Hester and James kissing each other – or did *she* just try to kiss *him*?' asked Norva.

'Norva, I couldn't see, I don't know.'

'But what do you think?'

'Does it matter?'

'Yeah it totally matters!' said Norva. 'It could help us figure out if they were in on the note together, or whether it was a solo mission.'

She had a point.

'OK, I think Hester kissed him. He kissed her back for a second, and then he stopped.'

'Hmmm,' said Norva.

'Does that help?' I asked.

'Not really.'

The lift doors opened on Floor 22.

'Right, wherever these keys go – we go,' said Norva.

'We not letting them out of our sight.'

I nodded.

We walked down the corridor to Flat 223.

'We need to somehow speak with Hester and James separately before we make an accusation,' I said.

Norva nodded.

She stood tall and knocked on the door. George answered. He closed the door to behind him.

'Tell me you've got them?' whispered George.

Norva jangled the keys in front of his face.

'Yesssss,' said George. He made a fist.

'Tell us you've found the original set, please?' I asked.

George shook his head.

'Trash,' said Norva in a low voice. 'But you know what – you did this whole investigation a solid by losing them.'

'I did?'

'Yes, we saw – well, we heard – Hester kissing James.' I said.

George's eyes grew wide. 'Are you serious? You ain't lying?'

We shook our heads.

'Ohhh – so that's where they went!' George put his hand to his chin. 'Oh! You reckon they put that note together… together?'

I shook my head. 'Evidence points to no. We don't

believe they're in a relationship anymore.'

'But they were kissing?' said George. 'I'm lost.'

'James isn't into it,' said Norva. 'Details to follow, let us in.'

George nodded and opened the door. He shouted down the hallway. 'Team – we have the keys. I repeat – we have the keys.'

A cheer rose from the end of the hallway. George looked at us and smiled. He beckoned us to follow him, and we did.

The crew – except Katarzyna, who scowled up at us from the sofa – were sat at the now cleared table. From clockwise: James, Simon, Hester, Afua.

'They've got the keys,' said George proudly. 'I told you.'

Norva held them between her thumb and forefinger. Hester, James and Afua reached for them. Norva snatched them back and clutched them to her chest.

'Pap – Joseph to you – takes safety and security very seriously here at The Tri,' said Norva. 'If he knew your keys were missing – with such an important celebrity here,' she smiled sarcastically at Katarzyna. 'He would shut down your shoot with a quickness.'

The crew groaned, but I nodded. This was true. Especially with the existence of the note. The shoot would be over.

'You can use the keys –' said Norva.

The crew cheered.

'– but we have to be with them at all times. We cannot risk this set being lost too – you lot would be in incredible trouble.'

Hester sighed. 'This shoot is an absolute farce.'

'But what choice do we have?' said James.

'You can always make the right choice, James,' said Hester.

Norva and I looked at each other. Katarzyna stared at Hester from the sofa.

She continued to stare at her as she stood up.

'No, you know what? said Katarzyna. 'The babies are actually right. For once. They can stay.'

34

'Kat, you sure you want them to stay?' Afua sighed. She reached for a bag of Beast Bites. She looked around at Simon, Hester and James for support.

It was not forthcoming.

Simon looked at the table. Hester and James looked at each other.

Of course they did.

'Very sure,' said Katarzyna coolly. 'Welcome girls.'

I did not feel the meaning in her words. At all. Neither did Norva, judging by her sideways glance in my direction.

Katarzyna gestured us towards the table.

'James, you were about to go through the stunt? Carry on.'

James looked up at Katarzyna.

His eyes said "really?" She stared back.

James stood up. He reached for a large chunky black case, defeated.

He placed it on the table and opened it.

Norva and I peered over his shoulders.

Inside, scattered on top of his equipment, were James' five newspapers – or what was left of them.

The titles and headlines from all the front pages had been ripped off.

Incrimination.

I reached for my phone immediately.

Norva and George gasped simultaneously. George, realising he was drawing attention to himself, pretended to cough. Afua stared at James. James looked at Katarzyna who gathered them quickly and threw them on the floor. She smiled at the group.

Hester and Simon looked at each other.

'Why are you all being so weird about scrap paper?' said Hester. 'Can we get on with it?'

'Please,' said Simon. 'I need to run through this so I can set up the speakers, and now the lights, too.'

James scratched at his neck. His pale face shone with a thin film of sweat. His hands trembled as he removed the equipment from his case.

'Rope. 20 meters. Not too much, but enough to wrap around me, and to attach to Kat. A new harness. That will hold your weight, Kat. The old one's here too as a back-up, in case we need it. Very unlikely though.'

Hester reach out to touch the new harness. 'Will you see this under her outfit, though? It's so ugly.'

James slapped Hester's hand away immediately. 'No one touches the harness but me, okay?' He looked around the people at the table. 'That goes for everyone. Safety. First.'

Hester stood back. 'Yeah, yeah, I get it, I'm just saying –'

'Stop saying,' said Afua. 'I'm trying to listen and learn here, thank you. Continue, JPD.'

'Alright,' he said. He pointed to a range of metallic clips. 'Belay devices, to help us control the speed of the drop. Rope protector in case the bricks are particularly sharp up there, or if there are any wires.'

'You haven't been up there at all?' said Hester.

'Hester, I'm going up soon, now we have the key.'

'Safety first, right James?' Hester said. 'Or something else on your mind?'

I looked at Norva. Her head swung between Hester and James. Her mouth hung open.

She was loving this.

James continued.

'Carabiner clips – both regular and locking models. We might not need them, we'll see. So that's it.'

'Well, not quite it,' said Hester. 'I've decided on the

shot – Simon will help me set up the lights. Unfortunately Leigh, my light guy, can't make it today. He's sick. So Simon – along with his shadow – is doing that plus capturing ambient audio.'

George nodded. 'On it, boss.'

'I'm going to do make-up,' said Afua.

Hester sighed. 'You didn't hire someone specifically? It's not like your team is short on money!'

Afua waved her hand. 'I know what I'm doing, I'm ready to serve looks. My YouTube tutorial game is strong.'

'Wow. A true professional,' said Hester sarcastically.

Afua snapped. 'Hester, do you want to be here or not?'

'Good question,' said Hester. 'I signed up to this job so long ago. Things have… changed.'

The room was silent.

George clapped his hands. The tension broke in the room. 'This is going to be madness!'

Norva nodded.

'It's beyond sick,' he continued. 'Amazing.'

'What time will you start?' I asked.

'Seven,' said Hester. 'I want to get up there now, set up, break for food, and then begin.'

'Ah, okay,' said Norva. She coughed. 'That's going to be tight – we have other business to attend to between six and seven.'

She looked at me. I rolled my eyes.

'Fine!' said Hester through tight lips.

'It will have to be,' said Norva. 'It's not like you have a choice, really.'

Hester glared at Norva.

'Right, everyone – food then?' said Katarzyna. 'Bermuda's? I could actually do with a drink to be honest.'

'Drinking before a shoot, Kat?' asked Afua. 'You sure?'

'Relax, doll. I'll have just one –'

'Yeah – it's never one is it? It's one times ten,' said Afua.

'You eat. That's fine. We're going to the roof,' said Hester. 'James, Simon, George – let's go. I need you.'

The group gathered their coats.

'Everyone be back here for six thirty,' said Hester. 'Please.'

35

Norva and I walked quickly ahead of James, Hester, Simon and George.

Down the corridor to the stairwell, and then up the 15 steps to the roof.

James carried his case. Hester's camera was slung around her neck. Simon and George carried a large speaker each.

'Business to attend to, Norva?' I said in the lowest of voices.

'Yep, we have to wrap up Trick or Treating real quick.'

'There's no "we" in Halloween, Norva' I said.

'Erm, there literally is,' she replied.

'You know what I mean.'

Norva laughed. 'Don't worry, clear your mind of that – focus on the now. Have we learned anything?'

'It's looking unlikely that Hester's involved in the letter,' I said. 'No clear proof. There is something between her and James but –'

'– it's not the note. I agree,' said Norva. 'She wasn't fazed by those papers at all.'

'Could she be playing it cool?' I said.

'Hmmm, nah, I'm not getting 'play it cool' energy from her.'

'So, it's just James then?' I said.

'I think so.'

'You think? You're not feeling the answer somewhere in your body somewhere?'

'Funny. But yeah, something's off.'

'OK – if you're right – that something is wrong – there are two scenarios at play here. James has either working with an accomplice – or he's been framed.'

'Yes, sis,' said Norva. 'I just got cold shivers at both of those hot suggestions.'

'So while we're up here, let's see if we can figure out which one it is and take it from there.'

'Yep,' said Norva. 'Stunning plan.'

We arrived at the door. The crew stood behind us on the steps in single file.

'Today please?' said Hester. 'While I still have a sliver of natural light?'

'Hold on, just getting the keys,' said Norva. She dug into the pocket of her jacket.

She put the correct key into the door, unlocked it

and pushed it forward. Diminishing light filled the dark stairwell. 'Welcome to your set!' she said enthusiastically. Her arms wide open. 'The Roof!'

Even though it was just one floor higher than our flat, the openness made it feel a thousand miles higher. I wasn't afraid of heights, but I held onto the door for a little longer than I would care to admit.

James had no such concerns. He wheeled his case to the edge of the tower. The edge that faced into the other two towers. The Rec – the all-weather pitch here – and The Gardens below us, between them.

'Wow,' said George. 'I've never been this high, this is crazy!'

'That's why we have to take extra precautions,' said James.

He opened his case and laid out his items.

Rope. Harness. Belay devices. Rope protector. Carabiner clips.

Simon and George positioned their speakers under Hester's direction.

Norva skipped around the roof.

'Whooooo!' she screamed. 'Can't nobody tell me nothing when I'm up here!' she shouted.

'Be careful,' James snapped. 'It's not safe up here – it's not a playground.'

James knelt on the ground, near the edge of the tower.

Norva walked over to him. I followed.

'So, James,' she said. '*Expedition: Intolerable*; we want to see it!'

'You should see it – it's a 12A, so you should just about get in without your Dad. It's good.'

'Cool cool cool,' said Norva. 'We were thinking about your reviews –'

'Hmm. Yeah. What about them?' James slipped the rope protector onto the rope.

'Do you keep them? Your reviews? In like a scrapbook?'

'Yes absolutely,' said James.

'Could we see them?' I asked.

'Erm, no,' he laughed. 'I'm clearly busy,'

'Okay – we'll get our own. Reviews are normally at the back of a newspaper, right?' I said.

'Yep,' he snorted. 'It's not breaking news,'

'That's what I thought,' said Norva. 'That's so funny.'

'What is?' he asked.

'Well, when we saw your papers just now, it was the headlines and titles that were missing.'

36

James's eyes grew large. First they looked at Norva, and then at me.

She walked towards James, closer to the edge of the roof.

He quickly looked at the rope in his hands. He pulled it through his palms. He pulled it tight.

'Why would anyone take the headlines from a newspaper, Norva?' I asked. Every word dripped with faux innocence. I was not as good an actress as Norva – she was definitely the star of our show – but I tried my best.

'Who knows?' she said. 'If the reviews aren't on the front, I'm not sure. Unless…'

'Unless what?' I asked.

Norva laughed. 'No, it's too ridiculous.'

'No, go on,' I said. 'Unless what?'

'Unless someone was making one of those old-timey threatening letters.'

'Like the ones from films set in the 80s?' I said.

'Yeah,' Norva laughed. 'But that's just wild – I mean, who would do that?'

'Yes – it's a lot of effort for such little gain – and they're so incriminating – the police can get so much DNA from those.'

'Can they now?' said James. He was playing it cool, but the panic was evident in his voice.

I looked at Norva. She nodded.

Got him.

'Oh yeah,' she said. 'Our friend – she used to live here – is a Police Officer. She says she can pretty much paint a portrait of a suspect once they're done running their tests.'

Our friend Katie Smyth has never said this.

James looked up. 'Yeah right,' he said. 'Anyway, I don't know how those papers got there. That's not where I left them last night.'

Norva looked at me. I gave her a confused look in return.

Maybe we didn't have him after all.

'They were somewhere else last night?' I said. 'Where were you?'

'Am I under arrest or something? Why are you asking me all these questions?'

'It's good to ask questions!' said a voice behind us. Simon. He angled a heavy speaker into place. 'How will they learn, if you don't share?'

'Preach!' said George. I'm learning so much today.'

He looked at Norva and gave her a sly thumbs up.

James sighed. 'And I'm just trying to concentrate.'

'Same,' said Hester. 'I don't know what you've got me into here, James. Next time, we do this differently.'

James attached a carabiner clip to the belay loop on the harness. 'I don't think there'll be a next time.'

37

17:52

60% charge.

Norva and I ran across The Tri from Corner Three to Corner One. We had locked the door on Corner Three's roof. The crew had dispersed, taking George with them for an early dinner. The keys jangled in Norva's pocket.

I used my set to let ourselves into our flat.

'Ringo?' Norva shouted. 'Ringo, I need you!'

Silence.

'Ringo? Smoked ham, Ringo!' Norva shouted.

The sound of a small animal jumping from the sofa and trotting up the hallway quickly followed.

'Always works!'

We let ourselves into our room. I sat by our computer. Norva opened her wardrobe. Ringo jumped on my bed.

'I don't feel like we have sufficient evidence to make a firm call on James' framing/accomplice situation.' I said.

'Nope,' said Norva. Her head in the wardrobe. 'James

looked well nervous when we spoke about the letter to him – superb acting by the way. So I think we're clear it's him.'

'Thanks. He said he didn't leave those papers in his case, though.'

'It's so strange,' said Norva. 'Does he have an accomplice then?'

'And if so, is that accomplice framing him?' I said.

'Ooh, this thing runs so deep,' she said. 'It's got layers like an onion, this one. Ringo – ham!'

Ringo jumped off the bed, and into Norva's wardrobe.

I looked at the files. 'When we go out I think we should pay a visit to –'

'– Sandy in Corner Two? Ben and Diana's neighbour? Without a doubt.'

Great minds.

'Ok, Nik, shut your eyes. You ready for me, the Halloqueen?'

I sighed. 'I would rather look at the files to be honest, Norva.' I stared straight ahead at the computer.

'Don't be ridiculous, check me out!'

I spun round on my chair.

Norva was wearing a short white curly wig. A black boxy dress. A string of pearls around her neck. Fake blood dripped from her mouth.

She held Ringo under her left arm. A tiny deerstalker hat on his head. A small string of pearls replaced his collar. Fake blood around his snout. Pap would not be happy when he saw that.

In her right hand she carried a notepad and a pen.

'So?' she asked expectantly.

'So, what?' I replied.

'So what? Who do you reckon we are?'

'Zombie grandma and her zombie Sherlock dog?'

'Close… we are… dun dun dun… Aaagh-atha Christie and Ringo here is Wagatha Christie.'

'Congratulations,' I said.

'That's it? That your reaction. You're beyond sour,' she replied.

I shrugged. She shrugged back at me.

'Ready to go?'

I hesitated. I knew we had to go out. I knew that Halloween was the perfect cover for investigation. It just felt so, so silly.

'Come on,' she whined. Norva kneeled next to me. 'Think about it. We'll do a couple of flats in Corner One. Get over to Sandra's. Maybe Bermuda's.'

'Hmmm.'

'We'll get a bit of money, pounds for the Peaks.'

'I really don't like it,' I said.

'Please sis,' Norva begged. 'I know it's stupid to you, I know it's childish. I just feel this is like my last chance, you know, before the true meaning of Halloween goes out the window –'

'The true meaning of Halloween?' I began.

'Come on Nik, it used to be a nice thing we did with Mum, and then Katie. Just do it with me, one last time.'

She looked at me with moist eyes.

To my shame, I don't remember our Mum. But I remember going with Katie. I hated every moment and was always glad to return home. I do, however, remember it being the highlight of Norva's year, though. I looked at her again. Her bottom lip trembled.

'Are you faking emotions again? To manipulate me?'

'No, not this time,' she said. A tear rolled down her face. 'I wouldn't scam my own sister!'

I was 65% convinced she was telling the truth.

I pushed myself away from the desk. 'Alright,' I said.

'Yay!' she said.

A little too cheerfully.

38

Corner One reactions to Norva and Ringo's costume were mixed to negative.

40% of visited residents were either confused or offended.

50% said nothing.

10% laughed in her face.

Our total takings:
- £4.33
- A five euro note
- two sour lollipops

A degrading experience, overall. 2/10.

'Maybe Corner Two will treat us better and respect my vision?' said Norva. She topped up the fake blood around her and Ringo's mouths. Ringo lapped at the sweetness. I recoiled.

'Not all of Corner Two, please – just the eleventh floor.'

'Just the eleventh,' Norva nodded. 'I hear you,'

We got into the lift. I pressed button 11.

'Okay, Ben and Diana live at 113. Let's not knock there.'

'Why not?'

'I don't want to remind them of what we did this morning… you do remember this morning?'

'Yeah, maybe. But if they see me in this costume, they'll think I'm cute and it might disarm them and we can get more intel and —'

'Norva, please. Focus.'

'Alright, alright.'

The lift stopped.

'Right, there's 111.'

I knocked at the door.

'Trick or treat!' said Norva brightly.

I put my finger to her lip.

'That puts people off, Norva — just wait until they get to the door OK?'

She rolled her eyes. 'Alright, alright.'

Footsteps from the hallway.

It opened slightly. A small, brown skinned boy appeared. Black hair. Brown eyes. Blue pyjamas. He looked at us with one eye through the crack in the door.

'What you want?' he said. He looked down at Ringo.

'Your dog looks stupid.'

'Rude,' said Norva. 'Trick or treat?' She looked him up and down. 'Why are you in your pyjamas already? Do you go to bed at like four or something? Are you a baby?'

'No. I'm not, I'm eight. Why you dressed like your dead nan?' replied the boy.

Norva chuckled. 'Where are your parents?'

'As if that's your business,' he snorted. 'I don't tell strangers our business.'

'Does Sandra live here?' I asked, cutting in. 'Is Sandra your mum?'

The boy roared with laughter. 'Sandra ain't my mum! She lives next door.'

Norva lowered her voice. 'What do you know about her? Give me two facts.'

'Why? What's it worth?'

'I'm working on a trick,' said Norva. She rummaged in her pocket. 'I'll give you these lollipops if you help me.'

'Hmm, alright.'

'Don't tell lies now, I know where you live,' said Norva with a smile.

'Alright, alright, OK, Sandra's favourite colour is pink. Her dog Bessie died last year. Big black and white one. Dalmatian.'

'Telling the truth?'

'Yeah, now give me the sweets.' He jumped up and snatched the lollipops from Norva's hand. He unwrapped one immediately.

'Thank you,' I said. 'Have a good evening.'

'Whatever, go away,' he said. He narrowed his eyes at Norva, popped the treat in his mouth before shutting the door.

'That kid was next level,' said Norva. 'I kind of loved his vibe.'

'You would. Right, 112.' We walked 10 steps and I knocked at the door.

The sound of shuffling behind it. It opened. A woman. 60s. Tall. Thin. Tan. A fake deep tan. Fluffy pink dressing gown. A pink blanket wrapped around her shoulders.

The boy was telling the truth about her colour preferences.

'Hello,' she sniffed. 'Cute dog! How can I help ya?'

'Trick or treat!' said Norva brightly.

The woman laughed. Her voice was hoarse. 'Well, I've been sick for days so no treats here, I'm afraid.' She coughed. 'Trick!'

'Alright,' said Norva. 'I can read minds!'

'Oh, you can?'

'Yep,' said Norva. She closed her eyes and put her hands to her temples. 'Your name is Cyn, Cynthia – no, no – your name is Sandra. It's Sandra! Am I right?'

Sandra's eyes grew wide.

'Yeah, it is! How did ya know?' She pursed her lips. 'Ya been spying on me?

'Nope,' said Norva. 'I can feel energies,' she replied. She pointed to me. 'This is my sister. She's got the gift too! Nik, show Sandra.'

I stared at Norva. She grinned back. I bit the inside of my lip. I put my fingers on my temples and closed my eyes.

'I know your favourite colour is pink,'

Sandra snorted. She patted her blanket. 'That's obvious.'

Norva laughed. 'My sister is rusty. Try again, sis. You can do it.'

I sighed. I kept my eyes closed. Mostly out of embarrassment and shame. 'Bessie, your Dalmatian was incredibly important to you.' I opened one eye.

Sandra stumbled in the doorway. 'Wow! My baby Bess? I miss her so much. How did ya know about her?' Her eyes filled with tears.

'Energies,' I said.

'And auras,' added Norva.

'What else ya got then? Quickly, as I need to lie down.' Sandra held her chest.

'I can see that you have a new special someone,' I said.

'A new love.'

Sandra smiled. 'You can see my Brian?'

'Yes,' I lied. 'He's a lovely… looking man.'

'I know! What a catch!'

Norva put her hands back to her head. Her eyes closed. 'I can see that you and Brian went out last night and came back around midnight.'

'Ah no,' said Sandra, deflated. 'Not us. I told ya – sick for days. No dates for me.'

'Maybe I'm picking up on your wishes,' said Norva.

'Maybe,' said Sandra. 'Or ya might be sensing other romantic energy from this corridor.'

I raised an eyebrow. 'Really?' I asked.

'There was a couple kissing and messing around here last night. 11:50. I know the time because I took my last tablets at that time. Young selfish lovers, making noise,' tutted Sandra.

'Did you see them?' I asked.

'Nah, just their backs – a little thin dark-haired girl with long curls dressed in black. She was with a taller man. They were in and out. I saw, through my peephole. I thought about calling the manager, but I don't want trouble – I'm too sick for that.'

'Thanks, Sandra,' said Norva. 'This was very cool. Send our love to Brian. '

'Will do,' chuckled Sandra. 'And protect that gift you have – and your blessed puppy. Give him a cuddle from me.'

Sandra closed her door. Norva looked at me.

'Long curly black hair, kissing a tall man at ten to midnight…'

'Katarzyna and James Paul Dean created the note and put it under Ben and Diana's door,' I said. 'Wow.'

'To quote you – evidence, fact, deduction,' said Norva. 'And now Kat is either being careless, or she's throwing her man under the bus.'

'Because she's upset about Hester?' I said.

'Potentially,' said Norva. 'Maybe –'

Oooooh Oooooh

Norva's phone.

'It's George. It's almost seven, and the crew need the key. We got to roll!'

'Right let's drop Ringo home, and go.'

'Go and confront James and Katarzyna now, yes,' said Norva.

'No, not yet,' I said. 'Wait until the shoot is over. They'll be in high spirits. We can do it then.'

'Oh that's dark, Nik, I'm well into that.'

* * *

19:01.

Norva put the key in our door, threw Ringo into the hallway and spun around.

'Let's roll out. Actually, wait – I need the loo,' she said.

Ringo ran down the hallway. I heard Pap's gasp, as Ringo jumped directly onto his lap.

'What's all this mess on your face,' he said to Ringo. 'Norva!' he shouted. 'What have you done to the dog?'

'Can't talk, Pap. Peeing!'

While Norva used the bathroom, I peered into the telescope and looked out across The Tri.

Candles in the windows.

Children carrying pumpkins in black cloaks. I angled towards Corner Two. On the ground, two bright spotlights beamed into the sky.

They were both cordoned off with a strip of tape. Like a crime scene.

I shuddered.

Not again.

'What you looking at?' said Norva behind me. She leaned to look in the lens. She stood up straight and touched my arm.

'Don't worry,' she said. 'It's not what you think it is. That's just to make sure people don't walk under the shot when they are filming. It would ruin it.'

'You sure?'

'Totally. It's fine.' She looked back into the telescope. 'Well, well, this is interesting though: who is that, up there?'

'Who, where?' I said, nudging her out of the way.

On the roof of Corner Three was a figure, wearing all black. The figure stood by the edge of the building. It was throwing a rope repeatedly over the edge and back up again. When it was satisfied, it turned and walked quickly to the door on the roof.

'How did someone get to the roof without keys?' I said. I stood up quickly. 'George didn't lose his keys, did he?'

'Oh my god, I swore he did. *He* thought he did – but this very much looks like they were stolen!'

'Who was that? Was that James?' I asked. I shook, my breath short, my chest tight. 'Was he touching the harness?'

'I can't tell – it could have been any of them!'

We looked at each other.

'We need to go. Now!' Norva said, grabbing my arm.

39

As we ran, Norva sent a message to George with a speed and accuracy I had never seen before.

I led her by the arm across The Tri towards Corner Three. She stared at her phone.

> URGENT! Who is in the green room?
> Need to know immediately.
> This is actually v srs now.

Oooooh Oooooh

Instant reply.

> Literally just me. Crew out and about.
> Tired of waiting. On their way back. What's happening?

Ring! Ring!

George.

'You're on speaker, alright, G?'

'Cool cool – what's happening?'

'So James Paul Dean created that note with an assist from Katarzyna.'

'Wait – what? Kat's in on it? Make it make sense!'

'We can't yet,' I said. 'But we're trying.'

'George – it gets worse, mate.'

'How so?'

'We reckon someone stole your keys. We just saw someone on the roof messing with the equipment!'

'No,' whispered George. 'This just got way more serious.'

I pushed the button for the lift.

'Right?' said Norva. 'Someone on the shoot is hustling, scamming, bamboozling you, mate.'

'I've been absolutely hoodwinked!' whispered George. 'Do you think James and Kat took them? The note and the keys have got to be part of the same plot!'

'We're not sure,' I said.

Trust no one,' shouted Norva.

The lift doors were opening.

Through them we heard singing.

'Gotta go!'

She quickly ended her call.

When every day you rise
Do you watch me fall?
You look back while you run
And see me crawl

TrojKat's words, but not TrojKat's voice.

A great voice. 8.5/10.

The lift doors opened fully, and we could see that the voice belonged to Afua. She stepped out. She was dressed head to toe in black.

She looked Norva up and down in surprise. 'So, that's the business you've been attending to?'

I had forgotten Norva was still in her Aaagh-atha Christie costume. I was already used to it.

'What are you supposed to be?' she said. 'Let me guess – an eerie aunty?'

'Nah – I'm Aaagh-atha Christie,' said Norva. 'I had a notebook with me, but it was long, I had to ditch it.'

'Aaagh-atha Christie,' chuckled Afua. 'That's actually brilliant, you know?'

Norva grinned. 'Yeah I know – she doesn't though,' She jerked her finger at me.

I shrugged and stepped into the lift.

'Heading back up? Good timing, we'll be ready to get going in a mo.'

'Did you find the other keys yet?' I asked Afua. I held the lift door open.

'Nope, they just straight-up disappeared – so weird.'

'Yeah that's weird?' said Norva. 'We just saw something super odd, too.'

'Oh yeah?'

'Yeah we saw someone on the roof just now.'

Afua clutched her chest. 'What?'

'Yeah, it's probably nothing – perhaps we were seeing things?' said Norva.

'What was this person doing?'

'Touching the equipment,' I said.

'You sure about this?'

Norva and I nodded.

Afua reached for her phone. 'I'll text the crew – see if they know anything about it. Don't say anything, when you get up there – I don't want to start a panic and delay the shoot. Was probably just James.'

Norva and I looked at each other. I turned to Afua and nodded. 'Where are you going anyway?'

'We're running low on Beast Bites,' she laughed. 'I have to pick up a packet or two. I thought I had more, but they've gone walkies.'

She began to sing again.

I've got to let you go
I need to be with me
A star is on its rise
Do you see?

'You have a really nice voice, Afua.' I said.

'Yeah, I didn't know you could sing?' said Norva.

'I'm not bad, I'm not bad. I don't have it though,' Afua said. She smiled. She threw up her hands. 'Kat's the star – I'm just here to make it happen.'

'Are you moving to New York with her?' I said.

Afua stood still. Her smile fell. 'She's going – I'm not. I'll see you up there.'

Afua paced quickly away, her phone in her hand.

We watched her as the lift doors closed.

'I don't understand,' I said. 'What is it? If you cannot define *it*, *it* doesn't exist.'

'Oh no, yeah it's totally a thing,' said Norva. 'It's a vibe, it's an energy, it's a way of life'

I shook my head.

'It's like this – I have *it*, and you don't, really?' she said.

'Is that an insult?'

'I mean, it's a fact, so no.'

'Okay,' I said doubtfully.

Norva laughed.

The lift doors opened.
The green room beckoned.

40

I checked my phone. 58% battery. 19:28.

The green room buzzed with activity. The crew were back, and like Afua, they all wore black. Any one of them could have been the person on the roof. Except for Katarzyna, who was a vision in white. A large white wedding-adjacent dress. She sat on the sofa. She played with her phone again.

George and Simon sat on the floor, untangling cables. George looked up and Norva and me. We exchanged looks and shrugs.

'Norva, that costume is really something,' George said, breaking the tension between the three of us. Simon looked up. 'Oh this is the Murderous Miss Marple outfit? It's pretty good!'

'Thanks,' said Norva. She wasn't listening to them. Her attention was drawn to the couple at the table.

Hester and James argued.

'That shot is going to look abysmal if you move the light there, James.' Hester pointed to the piece of paper on the table. 'It will cast shadows across her back and reflect into the windows. We'll possibly capture all the Halloween tat everyone's got everywhere here.'

'No, it won't,' said James. 'It will be fine. Trust me.'

'Trust you?' Hester spat. 'Not anymore.'

She was right not to trust him.

James sighed and stood up from the table. He walked to the bathroom.

Hester looked up at us. She narrowed her eyes at Norva and scanned her costume.

She reached across the table and opened a bag of Beast Bites. 'I hate Halloween,' she said.

'Same,' I said.

I liked Hester now.

'Who the hell schedules a shoot tonight of all nights?' she asked. 'It's full-on amateur hour here.' She shouted that statement in the direction of the bathroom.

Afua returned from Better Buy. She sat on the sofa next to Katarzyna, applying make-up to her face.

Was she going to say something about what we saw? Anything? I hoped so. I bit my lip. I stared at Afua until she met my gaze.

'Afua, did you tell everyone —' I began.

188

'– everyone to have a great shoot? Yeah!' said Afua. She stared at me and shook her head. I gulped. 'Everything is fine – look at Kat's make-up – what do you reckon?'

We looked over.

Thick black make-up not only around her eyes – but between her eyes, and round to her temples. Pale lips.

Katarzyna looked like a futuristic racoon.

'It looks… great,' was all Norva could muster.

She hated it. I could tell.

Hester laughed. 'It looks terrible. Truly.' She threw her hands in the air. 'This truly is the circus, and all of you are clowns.' She turned and looked out of the window.

Afua glared at Hester. She then looked around the room for support. She didn't find it.

Simon looked at the floor.

'It could work, it could work,' murmured George, his hands to his face.

James Paul Dean walked over. He lightly touched Kat's face. He moved her chin, left and then right. She smiled up at him. He closed one eye.

'I love it,' he said. 'It's a look to die for. Let's go.'

41

Katarzyna stood at the very edge of Corner Three.

Literally on its cusp.

I thought back to Hester's comment. She was right, this concept was not nuanced at all.

James stood close to Katarzyna. Her phone was in her hand.

He pulled the harness tight around her waist and made sure it was secured around her thighs.

There was a small hole at the front and back of her dress. James clipped the carabiner clip to the harness and fed his rope through it.

'Is that all right?' I asked James. 'It's not broken, is it?' I peered over his shoulder. My heart thumped.

James gave me a strange look.

'Double check that kit, please,' shouted Afua. 'Make sure it's safe.'

'I have, Afua, and it is – I got your messages.'

James looked over at Norva and me with narrowed eyes.

Afua had clearly told him about what we had seen – or thought we had seen. I was reassured. My heart beat a fraction slower. I exhaled.

He turned back to Katarzyna and put his hands on her shoulders.

Katarzyna breathed deeply and closed her eyes.

'It's going to be fine – I've got you,' he said, quietly.

'Yeah we know,' whispered Norva next to me.

'Ready?' said James.

Katarzyna nodded. She looked into her hands. She used her face to unlock her phone. She turned to Norva. 'You want a job?

Norva nodded quickly. She stood tall. 'Yes I do, Kat.'

'It's still Katarzyna to you. But get some shots for me? I'll put them on social later.'

She threw her phone. Norva caught it confidently.

Norva squealed and looked at me. She was delighted. Finally acceptance, of sorts.

'Will do!' Norva shouted back.

We all inched closer to the edge of the building.

Hester turned to Simon. 'Simon – music!'

Simon nodded. George placed the headphones that were around his neck over his ears. He picked up a large microphone – covered in Simon's 'scarf' – on a large stick and held it in the air.

Hester lifted her camera to her eye and stood directly behind Katarzyna.

Cusp came through the large speakers, loud and clear.

Norva smiled, she nodded her head, and mimed the lyrics silently, mirroring Katarzyna.

With her back to us, Katarzyna stepped off the building and suddenly she was gone.

Norva gasped and clutched her chest.

James held onto the rope and pulled it towards him. He barely broke a sweat.

Hester leaned over the edge, her camera leading the way. We followed.

One floor down, against the brown bricks, Kat walked up the wall, her back towards us.

A pale vision against the dark sky.

Her long curly black hair whipped in the wind.

It was spectacular.

'Damn' said Norva, under her breath. 'That looked stunning!' she squealed. She squeezed George's arm. He smiled back at her in utter delight.

'That was truly next level,' he said.

Katarzyna reached the roof and jumped to safety.

Hester, however, was less than impressed. She let her camera rest against her chest. She raised her hands in the air in frustration.

'This isn't working for me at all,' she sighed. 'Through the camera, this just looks like a cheap stunt. It's adding nothing. Doing absolutely nothing. If we did it like this –'

Hester reached out to grab the harness around Kat's waist. Before she could finish her thought, James towered over her. His hand around her wrist. His knuckles bright white with the tension in his grip. He moved his face inches away from hers.

The crew was silent. They – along with Norva and I – watched the unfolding scene with open mouths.

'I told you,' he said, quietly and pointedly. The proximity of his breath to Hester's face made her fringe flutter. 'No one touches the harness. You hear me? No one – but me.'

I quickly glanced at Norva.

Hester stared back at James. Not a trace of fear or remorse in her eyes.

Katarzyna opened her mouth to speak, I assume to diffuse the situation somewhat. Before she could create words, James stared at her coldly. She closed her mouth.

Hester shrugged.

'Fine, James. I won't touch it,' she said. 'But I need you to change her position. We need to get the perfect shot – whatever it takes.'

42

'Let's go again,' Hester shouted. 'Into your new position, Kat. Face the camera. James?'

Afua was tense. 'Really? Are you *sure* we need this?'

'Yes, said Hester. 'Do you want this to be outstanding or not? I'm getting nothing from this shot, nothing at all. If you want emotional impact – you need to see her face.'

'But we haven't fully prepared for that angle,' said James. 'It's too risky.'

Katarzyna fiddled with the carabiner clips that poked through her dress. She looked across the city.

'Don't touch those!' James snapped.

'I'll touch what I want,' Katarzyna snapped. 'I'm not a baby. I want to do this. We're here already and,' she sighed, 'I can't believe I'm saying this, but Hester is right – if you don't see my face, what's the point?'

'We agree on something,' said Hester, looking at James. 'Thank you.'

Katarzyna pulled roughly at the harness under her dress and twisted it around her body.

James took a sharp breath. 'Don't do that!' he said. 'Please!'

Katarzyna narrowed her eyes. 'This is happening. Make sure it's safe, and let's get it done. I have somewhere to be.'

Hester sprang into action. 'Right Simon, George – queue the music.' She peered into Katarzyna's face. 'Afua – powder Kat's face please. Now.'

Afua stepped forward. She tapped Katarzyna twice around the waist, on the harness. 'You're going to kill it,' she said.

'I know,' said Katarzyna. 'When do I not?'

I looked over at Norva. She was frantically scrolling through the phone she was holding. Katarzyna's phone.

'Norva!' I whispered. 'That's illegal.'

'Give it a rest. She said "Get some shots" did she not? That's what I'm doing.'

Ding! Ding!
Ding! Ding!
Ding! Ding!
Ding! Ding!

My phone beeped four times. I scrambled for it in my pockets. Four messages from an unrecognised number.

'Nik!' said George. He flicked his hand at his neck and shook his head. He pointed to his headphones and then his microphone.

I nodded. 'Sorry,' I mouthed. I quickly silenced my phone.

'Ready to roll!' shouted Hester. She looked at Norva. 'If you want the shots Kat asked for, now's your chance,' she said.

We walked to the edge. 'Take some pics with your phone too,' Norva said.

I nodded.

James tightened the rope around his waist.

'I said ready!' shouted Hester. 'Positions please!' She stood behind James, camera poised. Norva stood behind her, filming from two phones.

Kat took a deep breath.

The crew – including Norva – nodded. George looked over at Norva and rolled his eyes, and smiled.

Katarzyna looked deeply into Hester's camera. She sung her lyrics with intent and purpose.

Don't
Break the bond
Don't
Cut the rope
Don't
Let me go
Cusp

On the word "cusp", Katarzyna stepped backwards off the building and I moved forward, my phone up. The lights on the ground floor beamed behind her. They framed her body, illuminating the contrast between her long black hair and her billowing white dress – which blew around her body in perfect pillowy clouds. Her face was still and serene. She looked beautiful, even with the heavy-handed make-up.

I forgot for a moment how much I disliked her.

James strained, gripping the rope.

I looked over at Hester, who was smiling triumphantly as she peered through her camera. She was right. So right. Katarzyna looked like she was moving in slow motion. Her hands and arms slowly sliced the night sky.

I looked over at Norva who was filming with Katarzyna's phone. She looked at me and mouthed 'wow.' She gestured at me to move closer to the edge.

The entire crew silently peered over the side.

Katarzyna hung from the rope. She was suspended in mid-air – at what seemed like a million miles from the ground. Her head, hair and arms hung back. Her eyes were closed.

'Now!' said Hester quietly. 'Walk up towards us, Kat.' Katarzyna opened one eye and smiled. She put her foot against the brick of the building. She slowly walked up, silently.

She reached the top.

'And cut!' shouted Hester, before Katarzyna had put her feet on the ground.

'See I told you it would be fine!' said Katarzyna from where she was balancing at the edge. She looked at me. 'I –'

Katarzyna never finished her sentence.

A sudden, snapping noise.

I looked at her face. Katarzyna's face. I'll never forget it.

It contorted into a rapid range of emotions.

Confusion. Shock. Horror.

She knew what was coming.

Her inevitable end.

She swayed. She grabbed at her waist. She fell backwards off the roof.

'No!' cried James Paul Dean. 'No!'

He was falling too, his face heading for the floor. The rope in his hands loose and broken.

No harness at the end of it.

No Katarzyna at the end of it.

His face changed, too. It twisted into a shape that I didn't think was humanly possible.

Instant, infinite grief.

Norva was on her knees, grabbing at George's ankles.

George stood still. His mouth agape.

Simon breathed heavily, his chest rising and falling rapidly. Hester shook, her camera trembled in her hands.

Silence. Then, a thud and screaming.

Afua screaming.

Her scream was endless, but it was memory of the thud that curdled my blood and twisted my stomach. It implanted itself in my brain, never to leave.

'No, no, no!' shouted Afua in my ear.

TrojKat was dead. Definitely.

Murdered. Certainly.

31/10. 19:56.

I dropped my phone.

43

An incredibly shocked Hester stepped forward, tears in her eyes. 'This set is shut down,' she shouted over Afua's screaming. 'I repeat, this set must be shut down.'

That statement felt utterly pointless.

She bit her lip. She reached for her phone.

James, with his end of the rope still around his waist, stood at the very edge of the tower. Frozen. His face pale moon white. I could see he was daring himself to look over the edge but pulled back at the last moment – before he could see her body. He sat down at the edge of the building. His hand flew to his mouth. He retched. He wiped his lips. He screamed.

A guttural scream that came not from his throat, but possibly from the pit of his stomach. Or from the centre of his heart.

He stared at Norva.

Hester peered at the footage she had taken. Searching

for clues? A reason?

The perfect shot?

She was trying to stay calm, but her twitching suggested otherwise. As she looked, she shook.

Afua comforted Simon, who sobbed hard. His hands above his head, fingers twisted in his hair. He stared down at her with red rimmed eyes. 'I can't believe this! I can't believe this. She's gone? Kat's gone?' he screamed. 'Why her? Why?' Afua rubbed his shoulders. Tears ran down both their faces. 'She's was an absolute legend – and now she's gone? Just like that?'

Afua looked at him. 'What do we do?' she said. 'What do we do?' she shouted. 'What do I tell Ben and Diana? How do I tell them?'

Ring! Ring!

My phone. I looked at the screen.

Pap.

Screams rang out from below – then laughter.

James stood up. 'I have to see her, I have to cover her up, she can't be left like that. No!' He paced towards the doorway to the stairs, but Afua stopped him. He looked at her intensely, as if he was searching for answers in her eyes.

Pap. He must know by now.

I answered.

He knew.

'What happened? What happened?' Pap shouted. I moved the phone away from my ear. 'What the hell happened up there? Tell me this is a prank and part of their film – tell me! Nik? Are you OK? Are you safe? Where's Norva? Is George with you?'

'Pap, it's not a prank, not a prank at all!' I said.

I burst into tears.

'It's really bad, really bad. I saw her face. I saw everything. She was looking in my eyes.'

'I'm on my way,' said Pap. His voice trembled. 'What happened? What happened, Nik?'

'I don't know, Pap,' I said. 'There was some kind of… accident.'

I looked down at Norva. She was already looking up at me.

We both knew I was lying.

44

Between the wailing, the trembling and the heavy breathing, what was most noticeable was the sound of multiple phones receiving a multitude of messages and calls.

The word was out. The news had travelled at light-speed.

George cried into his phone. He was talking to Nina.

Simon hugged his microphone and cried silently into his scarf. His shoulders moved up and down rhythmically.

James clawed at his face and neck and scratched at his scalp. The rope still around his waist. He took deep breaths. He started shouting. 'Why did I let her do this? Why didn't I stop her? I knew changing the stunt was dangerous!'

Hester replayed her footage over and over again. A silent tear rolled quietly down her face. She sniffed and wiped it away.

'Nobody let Kat do anything,' said Afua. 'She did her own thing. You didn't own her.'

'I should have said no!' James shouted. 'I shouldn't have let you get so close to her, Hester. You're always pushing people to their limits.'

Hester stared at James. 'How dare you!' she shouted. 'This is somehow my fault? You pushed me away! I've been trying to be professional, but you keep saying things like this!'

'You need to shut up,' James said quietly. 'You need to shut up! This is your fault! Yeah – I'll say it! Your fault! We had the shot, it was a wrap. But no – you had to have it your way!'

'Stop! Stop it now!' said Afua. 'This was an accident. Something was wrong with the rope or the harness –'

'No!' James said. 'No! No! It cannot be. It cannot possibly be. They'll blame me – they'll think I did this! Me! I would never. I loved her. I wouldn't, I wouldn't!'

'You *loved* her?' spat Hester. 'Really?'

'No one loved her more than me,' said Afua flatly. 'She was my everything.'

'Wanna bet?' said James. 'You don't know anything about her. About us.'

'I knew you had some puppy love crush on her,' Afua snorted. 'But who didn't? Everyone does!'

'Oh no – it was more than that. We were engaged. We were going to tell you all tonight – after we told her parents.'

Hester mouth flew open. 'I don't believe you. You are *lying*!' she choked out. 'We only broke up a month ago!'

James shrugged. 'It's the truth.'

Hester staggered backwards in shock.

Simon spoke up. 'Everyone, stop,' he sobbed. 'This is our friend. Our friend! And now she's gone in this tragic accident and I –'

'Was it?' said Norva from the ground. 'Was it really a tragic accident?' She asked, emphasis on the last two words of her sentence. She looked around at the group. She started sobbing. 'We just saw her die!' she shouted. 'I can't believe this!'

I pulled Norva up into a hug and hissed in her ear. 'Wait, wait wait, Norva. Facts, evidence, deduction – remember. I know this is crazy, and we really have a case, but you need to calm down, before anyone does anything – anything else – they may or may not regret.'

She pulled away from me.

She nodded.

She looked at the crew. 'I'm sorry,' she said. 'I'm just so shocked. We all are. I agree, Simon. What a tragic, tragic… accident.'

45

This was of course no accident. No way. 0% chance.

That easy case we had before – the one where were investigated a tacky retro note? That was over.

Upgraded. To murder. We potentially stood next to a murderer – or a pack of them.

Was it the person who had helped Kat send the note? The person who touched the harness last?

Did James do this?

Was it the person who thought they were closest to her? The person who would be left behind once Katarzyna moved to New York?

Did Afua do this?

Was it the person who would do anything for the perfect shot? The person who was still in love with her ex-boyfriend, the victim's fiancé – apparently?

Did Hester do this?

Was it the person who has known her since sixth form? The only sound person in the crew – to borrow a pun from George?

Did Simon do this?

I wasn't certain about any of it – apart from the fact we needed to move. Move quickly.

Analyse the evidence. Gather our thoughts. Look at the note.

I moved closer to Norva and George. 'The police will be here any moment,' I said in a low voice. They're going to want to talk to the crew – once they've preserved the scene and identified Katarzyna formally.' Norva nodded. 'Yep, the feds will be asking questions any second.'

'The police are going to want to talk to us?' said Afua in my ear. I jumped. She stood directly behind me.'Yeah, you're right. Course they will. They should! We should be sticking together right now. Getting on the same page.'

'Getting on the same page?' said Hester. 'What's that supposed to mean? I'm going to tell them everything I know. I cover for no one.'

'I didn't mean it like that,' said Afua. She rubbed her head. 'Look, I don't know what I'm saying – there's nothing to hide here.'

'Right,' replied Hester. 'So I'm going down there.'

As Hester pulled the door to the staircase open, she gasped and jumped as a tall figure stepped through the frame.

Pap.

He pushed past her and sprinted across the rooftop to gather Norva, George and me into a hug. 'We're going,' he said. 'Now.'

***

'We all thought it was a Halloween prank at first,' said Pap. He opened the door from Corner Three to cross the Tri. 'Jane and I were out by the entrance of Corner One, handing out sweets. When Kat, you know…' he said.

We knew.

'Jane thought it was a joke. But I knew it wasn't funny. At all.'

Tears fell from Pap's face. He wiped them away quickly.

'I stood by her. Jane ran to get something to cover her. Someone walked by and said, "Cool dummy, Joe, that looks like an 'ex-wife' in that wedding dress". It was awful.'

I glanced over to where Katarzyna was lying, covered with a blanket.

Jane stood guard over the body, crying. She saw us with Pap and waved the saddest of waves. The spotlights aimed at the sky, illuminating the scene – already cordoned with tape – made Katarzyna's body look like it was on a stage.

TrojKat's final performance.

I looked over at George and Norva, who scanned the

scene.

They held hands. 'I can't deal with this NSquared,' George said. 'I can't take this, I can't. I'm going home.' George dropped Norva's hand and sprinted across The Tri to Corner One, without looking up.

Norva weakly called after him, but he was gone. She sighed, and looked at me with red eyes.

Norva went to open her mouth to speak, but a gasped cry sounded behind her.

The crew had come down to the scene, and what a scene they made.

James cried hysterically. The rest of the crew comforted him.

'This doesn't make any sense!' he screamed. 'None! I was the only person with access to the harness. I checked and I checked and I checked – no one went to the roof between the rehearsals! They couldn't have.'

'Not true,' said Norva quietly to me.

'I know,' I replied. 'I tried to say something! More than once. Afua messaged him.' My body shook.

Afua crouched next to Kat's body. She whispered something to her.

She put a small potted plant, a candle and the plastic pumpkin Norva bought from Better Buy next to her body.

'That's beautiful,' said Norva.

'Is it?' I said. 'The pumpkin is not appropriate and where did she get the plant and candle so quickly?'

Norva shrugged. 'Better Buy? The green room on the way down?'

'Yeah,' I sighed. 'But when?'

Ben and Diana ran to the scene. Their faces contorted by the pain. I was devastated for them. Their daughter. Gone. In an instant.

Diana, seemingly broken in every way, hobbled towards the body.

She stared at Afua. Her chest rose and fell rapidly. Her hands – balled into fists – trembled.

'I'm so sorry,' said Afua. 'I'm so sorry.'

Diana looked at Afua. Her eyes wild and wide.

'I told you it wasn't safe!' I told you! You saw the letter! Now my baby is dead. She's dead!' She screamed.

'No, Di – don't!' shouted Ben.

Afua stared at the Clarkes. Her bottom lip trembled, and she burst into tears.

'Come here,' said Ben. He drew both Afua and Diana into a hug. Together, they sobbed.

Rivers of tears.

Loud sirens, blue strobe lights.

The police were here.

46

Student and teacher. White and black. Chalk and cheese.

Officer Katie Smyth and DCI Alice Sharp.

Their car rolled onto The Tri. An ambulance trailed behind it.

'Bit late for that!' shouted someone in the growing crowd.

Officer Katie stepped out of the car, blue and white tape in her hand.

Katie Smyth. 26. Black hair. Blue eyes. Babysitter – well, she used to be ours, years ago.

She immediately set up a cordon and moved people out of the way. She shook hands with Afua and gave Diana and Ben a hug. 'I'm sorry,' we could see her say.

'She's getting much better at her job,' said Norva. She scratched at the white wig on her head.

It was true. She was.

We pushed forward through the crowd, towards the body, towards Katie.

She caught our eye. She shook her head in deep sorrow. 'I can't believe this!' she mouthed.

Norva started crying and shook her head. 'Me too,' she said. 'Me too.'

'The Alexander girls – how utterly surprising to see you here,' said a voice behind us.

DCI Sharp. Sharp by name. Sharp by nature. Sharp in tone. Sharply dressed.

Black trouser suit, black heels, black afro.

Norva gulped, and we turned around.

'What kind of costume is that supposed to be?' she said, staring at Norva.

'Aaargh-atha Christie,' said Norva. She looked at the floor in embarrassment.

DCI Sharp's face was softer than expected. Softer than any time we had seen it earlier in the year. 'It's certainly… something.'

'Alfa Sierra one, Alfa Sierra one, this is Oscar Tango three-one. Over.'

DCI Sharp's radio crackled into life. She turned it down.

'Halloween,' she sighed. She straightened her back. 'Who's in charge here?' she said.

I pointed her towards Katie and the crew. She walked over, her high heels clicking above the noise of the crowd.

Norva nudged me, and we followed behind. We loitered with intent, crouching behind the boot of the police car.

DCI Sharp joined Katie.

'DCI Sharp – this is Afua Martey, the victim's manager,' said Kate. She gulped. 'She's also her best friend.'

'Thank you, Officer Smyth,' DCI Sharp extended her arm towards Afua. She looked her up and down while they shook hands.

Katie's radio sprung into life.

'Kilo Sierra six-nine, Kilo Sierra six-nine, this is Oscar Tango three-one. Is it true about TrojKat? Over.'

Katie quickly silenced her radio. DCI Sharp glared at her.

'Ms Martey, we will be speaking to all of the crew in detail once we have preserved the scene and secured evidence, but for now I have a few immediate questions.

'Of course,' said Afua. 'Go ahead.'

I reached for my phone to take notes.

'Did you have a filming permit?'

'We didn't need one,' said Afua. 'We were a crew of less than five people, so we didn't need one.'

'What about George?' I whispered, looking at Norva. 'Doesn't he count?'

Norva shrugged.

DCI Sharp raised an eyebrow and looked at Katie. Katie grabbed her pen and stared intently at her notebook.

'Insurance – I'm assuming you have a policy in place?'

'Of course – we're insured by Tricilla Raworth – industry standard and recommended.'

'OK,' said DCI Sharp. 'And who was in charge of the stunt?'

Afua pointed.

'Him – James. James Paul Dean,' she said. 'An absolute professional. Just did all the wirework on *Expedition: Intolerable.*'

'Really?' said Katie. 'That film looks great. I'm seeing it next week.'

James looked towards the police. His face red, streaked with tears. His nose ran. Hester stood by his side, her hand on his arm.

'He looks terrible,' whispered Norva.

'Unsurprisingly,' I said.

'Is it though?' said Norva quietly.

'He didn't do anything wrong,' said Afua, as if answering Norva's question. 'James was all over the harness and the safety aspects – he wouldn't let anyone else touch it. Kat did the stunt once perfectly before the accident happened.'

'So what was different about the second time?' asked DCI Sharp.

'Well we – Hester – wanted to do it the other way round.'

'Hester is?' said DCI Sharp.

'Hester Bos. Our director,' said Afua. 'Hester!'

Hester looked up. She tapped James on his arm. She sighed and walked over.

'Hi,' she said. 'Here's the footage if you want to see?'

Hester handed the camera to DCI Sharp. Katie leaned over her shoulder and together they viewed the footage. DCI Sharp raised an eyebrow as it finished, while Katie blinked back tears.

'Thank you,' said DCI Sharp. 'Thank you all for your time. Please stay in the area while we conduct our investigation.'

'I understand you have a flat here in The Tri, given to you by management for use for the shoot?' asked Katie.

'Management,' whispered Norva. 'That's right, keep Pap's name all the way out of this!'

I nodded.

So did Afua. 'That's right.'

'Please remain there until you are contacted by us, for your own safety,' said DCI Sharp. 'I understand that your friend was somewhat of a celebrity? It's best to stay in the immediate vicinity as the news inevitably begins to spread.'

'Understood,' said Afua.

'Thank you,' said DCI Sharp. 'A word, Officer Smyth, by the car, please?'

'Move!' whispered Norva. We quickly crawled to the car's bonnet. 'I hope Kat can't see us doing this, wherever she is!'

Katie nodded at the group and followed the detective.

'This looks like one for the HSE,' said DCI Sharp.

I pulled my phone from my pockets and searched what that meant. Norva was looking at me.

'Health and Safety Executive,' I whispered. 'They investigate deaths at work.'

Norva nodded.

'Accidental death due to misadventure or manslaughter by gross negligence,' said DCI Sharp. 'That looks like what's happened here.'

'Well,' said Katie. 'We —'

DCI Sharp broke in. 'And honestly — with it being one of the busiest weekends of the year for the force, I wouldn't be opposed to that outcome. An accident is right.'

I stared at Norva. She stared back. Her chest rose and fell rapidly. DCI Sharp had failed us.

47

'This was no accident,' I whispered. 'Not a chance.'

Norva snorted. 'Absolutely not. Remember – Sharpy and Katie haven't been with them like we have – they don't know what we know.'

I nodded.

'We have to keep investigating and –'

'You're investigating?' said a voice behind us.

My heart decided to see what it was like to beat in my throat.

'What do you two girls have to investigate?' the voice snorted. 'And what are you wearing? You look a state.'

I bit my lip. We turned our heads slowly.

May Burton. 56. Bearer of bad views. Reporter with Cloud News. We knew her, unfortunately. From what happened with Hugo this summer.

We stood up to face her. 'I know you,' she said. She pointed her finger at us, and then her eyes suddenly widened. She smiled. She cocked her head to the right.

'How's your dad?' She laughed. 'That whole thing here over the summer was ratings gold – so thanks! Have fun with your little … investigation.' She blew a kiss and turned on her heel. 'Where are my lights?' she shouted with raised arms to no one in particular.

'If the media is here, that means the word is well and truly out,' said Norva. She quickly patted her body down.

'What?'

'Oh my gosh,' she said.

'What!'

'I still have Katarzyna's phone,' she said. Her mouth wide open. She pulled it out of her pocket, and it glowed in her face immediately.

Notification after notification after notification. Twitter, Facebook, Instagram, Snapchat, Tik Tok. Messages for Katarzyna – or mentioning Katarzyna – poured in.

She brought the phone to her lips and kissed it.

'I wonder if I can read these?' she said.

'Isn't it unlocked?'

'It was, earlier – but only because she gave it to me unlocked,' she said. 'How do you think I sent you all those messages – screen grabs of her last conversations with the crew, by the way – and yes, I deleted all trace of them, I'm not basic.'

I rummaged through my parka's pocket for my phone and searched my messages. Four messages from a now known, unknown number.

'That's really smart, Norva.'

'I know. I'm prepared. I'm basically a scout, but you know, not for camping or outdoor pursuits, but for any potential murders that may or may not occur around me.'

She peered at the phone.

She pressed the home button on the phone. It asked for a fingerprint.

Norva pressed her thumb onto the button. The screen shook. No access.

Norva tried her little finger. The screen shook again. No access.

She tried her other three fingers. The phone was now really locked. Disabled for ten minutes.

Norva sighed and threw her head back, her white wig slipping off slightly. She held the phone in her hand, and shook her head, holding onto her hair. 'Can you believe this is really happening?' she said. 'And on Halloween? It's awful. It's truly cursed. It's jinxed. It's cancelled, forever.'

'Part of me is glad about that,' I said. Norva smiled sarcastically at me. I put my hand on her shoulder. 'Let's move, see what else is happening.'

We ran from the car and ducked around the side of the ambulance.

May Burton had located DCI Sharp.

'Alice,' May purred. 'If you're here, well, then I know we're going to get something good. You got something good for me? Is it that singer that the kids love or not?'

'You have absolutely no respect, May,' said DCI Sharp.

May tilted her head and chuckled. 'You know me so well,' she said. May stepped forward. 'Come on.' She looked into DCI Sharp's eyes. DCI Sharp coughed and stepped back.

'I can confirm that there has been a casualty, Ms Burton. Katarzyna Clarke, professionally known as TrojKat.' DCI Sharp said quietly. 'We are investigating all leads and interviewing everyone who was with her before the time of death, but we currently believe that this is nothing more than a tragic accident.'

May clapped her hands. 'Excellent, I'll get the crew together.'

Before DCI Sharp could reply, someone ran forward and jumped between her and May.

A man, young. Eighteen? Chunky white trainers. Skinny black jeans. TrojKat t-shirt. He screamed at DCI Sharp with a tear-streaked face. 'Is it true? Is it true? Is she really dead?'

'Good god,' said May.

DCI Sharp shouted. 'Officer Smyth – we're going to need back up, and now! Get Burnett down here.'

'Understood,' Katie shouted. She nodded and reached for her radio. 'They're on their way, DCI Sharp' she said.

DCI Sharp walked the fan away from the scene, her hand on his back. 'You, and all your friends, need to stay back. If not, you are at risk of being arrested for tampering with the scene. So move. Now.' She demanded.

The fan moved away. He cried out, 'Someone's got to pay for this. We want justice!'

'Don't we all, honey!' laughed May. 'That's why we're here.'

DCI Sharp turned around to stare at May, and she caught our eye in the crossfire.

Our loitering ceased immediately, and we hurried away in the direction of the still-distraught crew, but May followed us.

'You!' she shouted. 'I know you!'

'Did she not just ask us that?' asked Norva.

But she wasn't talking to us. She was staring at Simon.

Simon did his best to avoid eye contact.

'Simple Sound Boy Simon!' shouted May.

Norva stifled a laugh. 'Burn,' she whispered.

'Well, well, well – look at you!' May grinned. 'Happy with your career choices now?'

'Yes,' Simon replied quietly.

'Well, if you change your mind, you can always come back to me? You weren't so bad.'

'No thanks,' he said. He turned away.

'Wait, Simon. While you're here, tell me what you saw – what happened?'

'No – no you don't,' said DCI Sharp stepping in between Simon and May. 'You talk to absolutely no one but me and my team. That clear?' She looked at Simon and the crew. They nodded. 'Go to your flat and wait for us there.'

Norva made herself known. 'I have keys, DCI Sharp,' she said. 'I can walk them up.'

DCI Sharp narrowed her eyes. 'Absolutely not. Get your father and go home – I don't want to see you anywhere near this scene. That clear?'

'Crystal,' said Norva.

We walked away.

Oooooh Oooooh

Norva reached into her pocket and pulled out her phone. 'It's George. He's waiting at ours. He's back in – our investigation continues.'

48

George had his back flat against our front door. He chewed his nails. His eyes were bright red.

He nodded at us as we approached him.

'I just need to do something,' he said. 'I close my eyes, and all I can see is that look of shock on her face as she fell. I can't believe it.'

I shuddered and shook my head. I thought back to Katarzyna looking me directly in the eye as she disappeared out of view.

Norva put her key in the front door and stepped into the hallway. George and I followed. We stood in the dark.

'I'll never forget it,' he said. 'That will stay with me for my entire life. I want to help – I need to help. She was a legend in the making. Whatever the truth is, it needs to come out. Quickly.'

I switched on the hallway light. George's face was streaked with tears.

Norva nodded and touched his shoulder. 'Completely concur, George. But are you sure you're cut out for this? For our investigation?'

'So ready. Never been more ready.'

'It's not fun, George.' I said. 'We have to gather facts, and then use those as evidence to come to the best conclusion. It's analytical work.'

'Well, you're not really selling it to me, Nik – but to be clear, I'm not looking for jokes right now, I'm looking for justice.'

I looked at Norva and nodded. She nodded back, proudly.

'You have my vote, George,' I said.

'And mine, without a doubt,' Norva said. 'Welcome to the team.'

I stepped into our bedroom, flicked on the light and shook our computer to life. 'Let's get going.' I sat down at the desk. Norva and George sat at the edge of her bed.

'So what happens now,' said Norva, 'is that Nik and I have a conversation about what happened, and Nik makes notes.'

'What, that's it?' said George.

'That's it?' Norva said. 'There's a lot to it.'

'I thought I didn't have it, Norva?' I asked.

'You said what?' said a shocked George.

'Forget all that,' said Norva. 'George, behold! Nik, is the original document open?'

I nodded. 'I'm updating the notes.'

'Excellent,' said Norva. 'OK, what do we do know?'

I took a deep breath. 'Katarzyna Clarke, aka TrojKat has died. Time of death. 19:56 on 31/10.'

'And how did she die?'

'It appears there was something wrong with the harness she was wearing during the stunt for her video shoot for *Cusp*.' I said. 'She attempted the stunt twice – one version with her back to the camera. When she attempted to recreate the stunt face-forward, it was successful, but –' I gulped. 'There was a malfunction as she was about to step back onto the building.'

'OK, "harness malfunction,"' said Norva with air quotes. 'Who had access to the harness?'

'Well,' I said. 'James was seemingly very protective over the equipment – and its safety.'

'Yeah, that's true!' said George, 'JPD was well strict about who touched it.'

'Right,' I said.

'But!' said Norva. 'We also saw someone dressed in black, creeping around the roof, touching equipment earlier –'

'Around 19:01,' I said. 'Through the telescope. We told Afua, who claimed she messaged the crew. I mentioned safety three times in the crew's presence.' I turned to George. 'The only way that person had access to the roof is by the key you... misplaced. Thinking back, do you have any idea who might have taken it?'

George slapped his fingers against his lips. 'You know what? I don't.'

'Well, where were they? Where were the crew? Where were you?' asked Norva. 'You need to give us details, you need to think!'

'Alright, alright,' said George. 'I'm trying.' He looked into the distance. 'Well, OK. It was just after one – as I just got there. The crew were sitting at the table, chatting through the stunt. Hester was cussing, saying that the shoot was basic, and she needed to get to the roof to set up.'

'OK,' I said 'This is good, George. Keep going,'

'Thanks, I will,' George said with a smile. 'The keys were sitting on the kitchen counter next to that flashing pumpkin you bought, Norva. You guys rang me and said you need a plan, so I grabbed them and put them in here.' George put both his arms into the front pouch of his hoodie.

'Then what?' said Norva. 'Did anyone see you?'

'Nah. I was slick, smooth and sly – everything a spy needs to be,' he grinned.

I rolled my eyes. 'Don't make me regret the decision to include you. Carry on.'

'Alright, Nik, relax. I snatched the keys and stood by the counter. Then Afua stood up to find them, realised they were gone and the whole crew stood up and started looking for them. The entire crew – not Kat though, she was lying on the sofa laughing at her phone – pushed around me looking for the keys. They were certain they were by the pumpkin.'

Norva sighed. 'So they were all hustling and bustling around you?'

'Yeah,' said George brightly. 'All over me.'

'So that means, in reality, any one of them could have taken the keys from you – without you knowing?' I said.

'Oh,' said a sullen George. 'Yeah, you're right. Easily any one of them.'

49

'That's alright, George, don't worry about it,' said Norva. 'Your mind isn't honed like ours yet. It will come. Let's think about the person creeping around up there around seven. Where was everyone around that time?'

'In and out,' said George. 'Everyone was busy preparing for the stunt, waiting on you both with the keys and coming back from Bermuda's – they do a food in there for future reference – or using the toilet. I couldn't tell you. I was concentrating on my job – untangling the cables for the speakers we were going to put up there. That job had me so focused, hypnotised. Simon says it's a key job for any intern to learn. He's a good one, that Si.'

George was no help.

I looked over at Norva.

She closed her eyes and shook her head quietly.

'Okay,' I said.

'Details are still murky. We were all on the roof, when it… happened. Let's think who touched the harness during that time. James, obviously. We also know Hester grabbed it once –'

'– and James lost it at her,' said George.

'She also said she needed the perfect shot – whatever it takes,' said Norva. 'Like a proper villain.'

'That doesn't make her guilty, though,' I said. 'Patience.' I thought back to the scene. 'Also, Afua put on a bit of powder on Katarzyna's face, then touched her waist. She might have touched the harness.'

'You noticed all that?' said George.

'Of course,' I said. 'I have to make sure we see everything.'

'You two are so thorough, it's unbelievable,' George said. He leaned forward.

'We try,' said Norva. 'So that means we know three people definitely touched the harness,'

'Afua, Hester and James,' said George. 'What about Simon?'

'You tell us,' said Norva, raising her eyebrow.

'Hey, I told you I'm not like you two! But – Simon was by me the whole time, apart from when he went to the bathroom.'

'How long was he in the bathroom?' I asked.

'Nik, I don't know – a little while? We had just eaten, so yeah number two length, not number one. Ten minutes?'

'At what time?'

'Just before you got here, after we got back, so like seven?'

'OK, good,' said Norva. 'We're getting somewhere. Aren't we?'

I updated my notes. I looked at all the information about the letter.

'This investigation has escalated so rapidly,' I said.

'Right,' said Norva. 'Back to basics. The note. Created and delivered by James and Katarzyna. Sandra confirmed that. Is James the murderer too? It would make sense.'

'But what if the letter and the murder aren't connected at all? Just because James is involved in the letter, it doesn't mean that he's the murderer.'

'Although it sure looks like it,' said Norva. She lay back on her bed.

'But they were engaged, Norva,' I said.

'But he only broke up with Hester a month ago. That's like no time at all,' said George.

'Yeah exactly, G,' said Norva. She sat up. 'This man is not legit. How's this for a theory – him and Hester, in it together, to get hold of Katarzyna's insurance coins. Their "break up" is a ruse.'

'But that doesn't make sense, Norva.' I said. 'He's not interested in Hester. We know this from his behaviour in Bermuda's last night, in Pap's office today, and again on the roof. He is not in love with her anymore. It's not checking out.'

'Okay,' said George. 'How about Hester by herself to get James Paul Dean back. Bumping off the competition?'

'Could be,' I said. 'But killing someone for love is very extreme, I –'

'Pffft,' Norva cut in. 'That literally happens every day, I'm afraid to say.'

Unfortunately, I realized she was very right.

I drummed my fingers against the desk. 'What about Afua?'

'Nah – she's her best friend, she loved her,' said George. 'She cared.'

'But what if she's upset about being left behind?' said Norva. 'I'd leave both of you with a quickness if I was TrojKat and NYC was beckoning. See ya, suckers.'

'Nice, Norva, really nice,' said George.

'What if Afua was jealous?' I said. 'Of Katarzyna's success?'

'Nah,' said George. 'I don't see it,'

'She's a better singer than her,' I said.

'Utter blasphemy!' shouted George. 'How do you know that? Afua hasn't even laid down any tracks, not that I know of anyway?'

'She's really good, George,' said Norva. 'We heard her singing by the lift. She was strong, even I have to say it.'

'No way!' said George. 'Even so, Afua wouldn't cut it anyway. She's not popstar material, she —'

'Why isn't she "popstar material" though, George?' said Norva. 'For real? Because she's got darker skin than Katarzyna? Because she's got kinky hair, and she's not skinny? That's trash.'

'No, no, no,' protested George. 'That *is* trash, I agree. To me, Afua just doesn't have… it.'

"It" again. I didn't understand it, but I was over it.

'Also,' George continued. 'Katarzyna was signed not only for her singing — but for the strength of her writing skills too.'

Norva looked at George through narrowed eyes.

Bloop! Bloop!

I reached into my pocket for my phone.

10% battery. I quickly plugged it into the charger by the

desk. On the screen, the notifications for that unknown number flashed up at me.

'Katarzyna's messages!' I said.

Norva put her hand in her pocket. 'And I still have her phone. We can try unlocking it now!'

But the battery was dead.

50

George jumped off Norva's bed.

'You still have Kat's phone, Norva?' He said. 'Is that a good idea?' He rubbed his head. 'Aren't the cops going to be looking it for it? Like, right this minute? They're probably tracing it to your flat as I speak, right? Right? That's what cops do isn't it? They're going to think we did it or something, aren't they? I can't do time – I ain't got the time!'

George smacked the phone out of Norva's hands. Norva and I watched it fall to the floor. We both looked up at George.

'I mean, if this was a film, George, the police would be tracing it, sure,' Norva said. She stood up. 'They would hack into a satellite, definitely.' She stepped next to George and pointed to our window. 'They'd be watching us in this room, right now.' She looked in his eyes. 'They'd be clicking enhance, enhance and then enhance again and they'd be watching you. Watching you freaking out.'

'For real?' said George. He backed himself up against the wall and fumbled for the door handle.

'No,' I said. 'And don't tease him, Norva.nGeorge, I fell for this once, I Googled it. The police don't have the resources or the time for that.'

'Norva!' George playfully punched her on the arm. She laughed.

'Are we going to discuss the evidence we actually have or not?' I said. 'Or are you just going to waste time?'

'OK, OK,' said Norva. She looked at George and rolled her eyes in my direction. 'Let's start your pal, G. Almost-silent Si,' said Norva.

'He seems like a nice person,' I said, 'But he is pretty quiet. What do we need to know?'

'He's cool, generous with his time. We've talked loads about the equipment and recorded little bits of audio to test the sound quality,' said George.

'You recorded "little bits of audio",' I asked. 'Of what, specifically?'

'Well, we captured bits of conversation in the green room and looped them, so he could show me what the sound recorder could do.'

'Do you have the files?' asked Norva.

'I never did – Si has them.'

'We need them,' said Norva.

I agreed. 'They could be crucial pieces of evidence.'

'OK fine,' said George. He dug his phone out of his jean pocket.

'What are you doing?' asked Norva. 'Tell me you're not straight-up texting him?'

'Erm, yeah?'

'Erm no!' she shouted. She slapped his phone out his hand. 'See we can both do that, can't we?'

'You can't text Simon,' I said.

'Why not?' said George.

'Are you serious right now?' said Norva. 'Do you want to die?'

'No!'

'If he's involved —' I said.

'— nah he's not,' George replied.

'He might be,' warned Norva.

'— he's going to know immediately, and you could be in danger. You have to be smart.'

'I don't know if I want to be in this club anymore,' said George. 'It's long.'

'That's definitely not the spirit, George' said Norva. 'Getting that evidence off Simon — sneakily — is on the list.'

'Katarzyka's and Simon's messages,' I said.

SOUND SIMON

You call Jessica?

Yeah last night their time
she said cool

said she would send
out an updated release

SOUND SIMON

thumbs up
And update the terms?

Yep

SOUND SIMON

OK cool.
Afua know?

In time, yeah

SOUND SIMON

Well, OK.
Glad that's now behind us.
See you at the shoot.

Certainly will

> I'll send over the flat
> number once I have it

> You're going to love
> George sweet kid

SOUND SIMON

> *thumbs up*

I leaned back in my chair. 'That's interesting,' I said. 'Jessica.'

'Yeah, the second time we've heard her name today,' said Norva. 'Diana said it. "Jessica from Arcadia", Katarzyna's record company.'

'They're going to send out an updated release?' I said. 'What does that mean?'

'George, this is your area,' said Norva. 'Speak up – have your moment.'

George took my phone and looked closer at the message.

'Could be a new track – or a press release,' said George. 'That's like a newsletter for journalists so they can write their stories.'

'And terms?' I said.

'Terms could be about a contract – maybe a change they made to one?'

'Why would they do that?' said Norva. 'Why would Arcadia want to change their contract with her?'

George shrugged. 'I have no idea.'

'Must have been serious. Afua doesn't know about it, and Simon's glad it's behind them now. That smells like beef to me,' said Norva.

'Maybe Simon's not so quiet after all,' I said. 'We're going to need your help on this, George.'

'No doubt. Katarzyna did say he was going to love me,' said George. 'She was right about that.'

'Blow your own trumpet, much?' said Norva.

51

'You notice anything with Hester in the green room, George?' I said. 'Was she acting strange or suspicious?'

'I mean, "strange and suspicious" seems to be her default setting, so…' said George.

'Nah, I don't think so,' said Norva 'She's just direct and knows what she wants – I'm into it, to be honest.'

'Well, she's not over James – I saw her giving him the eye in the green room,' George said.

'That tracks,' I said.

'And did you get vibes from him to her?' asked Norva.

'Hmmm, this is not my area of expertise to be honest,' said George. 'But I don't think so. He was just interested in his harness box, and in Kat's safety.'

'So, Hester wanted to do the shoot her way – she's still in love with James – and was trying to persuade him to go in her direction?' I said.

'Her "direction"? Nice one,' said Norva. 'How about this? With Kat out of the frame –'

'Ayyy,' said George. 'Metaphors!'

'– she could bring James back into the picture. Her picture,' said Norva.

George gave her a quiet round of applause. 'Beautiful.' 'Let's see the messages between Hester and Katarzyna,' said Norva.

'Are there any?' said George. 'They're not friends at all.'

Thursday 10:57

HESTER

answer your phone

Sorry – in studio.

What do you want?

HESTER

Details of your shoot!

HESTER

It's 2 days away.
I haven't been on set yet?
Have you seen the boards I created?

Thursday 11:32

HESTER

well?
are you going to call me
back or not?

Thursday 11:45

HESTER

seems not

Text Afua

HESTER

i've texted JPD –
the only one I respect in your
crew – an unprofessional mess

no – you don't call him
I'll talk to James

'Pretty tense,' said George.

'To be expected,' I said.

'I'm not in love with Hester or anything,' said Norva. 'But she has a point, no? If no one's spoken to her about the shoot, that super unprofessional.'

52

'I would pay to see the messages between James and Hester,' said George. 'The gossip.'

'Me too,' said Norva. 'It never works like that, though. We investigators have to weave that web together – answers are never passed to you on a plate.'

'Shame, because I'd eat them right up. Alright, let's see the messages from James,' said George.

Thursday 11:46

JPD

> Babe – why is no one communicating with Hester?
> Why am I involved in this?
> You know I don't wanna talk to her right now.

> I'm in the studio
> Also: this is Afua's job no?

This is why this can't work
She has to go

JPD

Totally. Afua needs to pull her socks up big time.
I LOVED Hester's concepts –
The video will be great.

You loved them?
You love her more than me?
You still into her?

JPD

Stop it, we're over!

Friday 18:32

JPD

Where are you?

In the shop here getting supplies for the project.

thumbs up
This is going to be great!
And what comes next will be even better.
:O

244

JPD

Changes!
I can promise that.

JPD

Did Afua sort the insurance?

JPD

Babe – did Afua sort the insurance?

JPD

I'm having second thoughts...

Ring! Ring! Answer your phone!

Saturday 00:35

That was so fun.

I can't wait to give them the whole
story tomorrow (well today)
143
<3 <3

JPD

143

'OK, wow – there is a lot in here,' said Norva. 'Well, well, well!'

'Loads' said George.

I nodded. 'I'll start. We can confirm that they were engaged and definitely in some kind of love,' I said.

'Yep,' said Norva, 'the engagement ring emoji, and all the hearts show that. What does 143 mean?'

I turned to the computer and searched. 'Yep, it's love – it means "I love you"; it's the number of letters in each word. I kind of like that,' I said.

'It's super tragic,' said George. 'You might as well just say the whole words. What else?'

'Well – James liked Hester's concepts,' I said.

'You mean James *loved* them,' chuckled Norva. She made kissing noises.

'On Friday, JPD talks about getting supplies for his project,' said George, getting the investigation back on track. 'Got to be the letter.'

'Definitely,' I said. 'The times match when we were in the shop with him – the last message is around the time Ben, Diana and Sandra heard and saw them in Corner Two.'

'You're right,' said Norva. 'Totally right. But the question remains – why would you send a threatening letter about yourself to your own parents? Potentially getting the police involved?'

'She wanted something to happen' said George. 'See what James said about change?'

'But what changes?' I said.

'Big enough changes to warrant freaking out her whole fam,' said Norva. 'And what about this bit about insurance?'

'James was pretty insistent on it,' I said. 'He messaged her twice about it.'

'Afua got the insurance, didn't she?' asked Norva. 'What did she say to DCI Sharp about it?'

George sat up. 'Sharpy's on the scene already?' he said. He shuddered.

Norva snorted. 'Of course she is. This is serious business. Sharpshooter was here with a quickness – and so she should. I would have been freaked out if they just sent Katie – no offence to Katie, obviously.'

George nodded. 'You're right.'

'Never not,' she said. 'But yes, Nik, insurance, what do we know?'

'She said she had insurance from Tricilla Raworth,' I said, checking my phone.

'Is that like a person?' said George. 'Like a super rich woman?'

'I'm checking.' I typed. 'Nope, it's a performing arts insurer.'

I typed some details into a form on their website. 'Using the information I have from the shoot – the time, the size of the crew, the risk – it seems that the insurance value would be three million pounds.'

'Three million!' shouted George. He rolled off the bed and onto the floor. 'That's a motive right there.'

Norva clutched her chest. 'Damn right, it is! Sis – does the size of the crew make a difference? Afua said five people, but she didn't count George when she was talking to DCI Sharp.'

'She didn't include me?' said George from the floor.

I turned back to the computer. 'No, it makes no real difference to the value.'

'Wait, so if Kat and James were engaged – or about to be married – then I'm guessing he would have a claim to the money?' said Norva.

'I don't think so,' I said. 'They would need to be actually married and have the certificate to prove it. The money would go to her manager though.'

The three of us were silent for a second.

'Let's keep looking at James,' I said. 'He says he's having second thoughts about something. Did you see that bit?'

'Yeah, I did,' said Norva. 'Sorry, I just got swept up thinking about all that money. And Afua.' She peered over my shoulder.

'The time is interesting, too,' I said. '18:32. Look – it's around the same time as the conversation we heard her have outside of the green room yesterday.'

'When she was saying "we have a plan" – she could have been talking about whatever it was they thought they were going to achieve from this letter?' asked Norva.

'The plot thickens,' said George, from the floor.

53

'So let's get to it quickly, does Afua say anything about the insurance in her messages to Kat?' asked George.

'Let's look,' said Norva. 'Show us, Nik. Let's see the messages between these two "best friends".'

Thursday 11:46

FUFU

She'll have to deal busy busy busy rn

I don't need this, Afua.

This is a job for the manager not the star.

I can't believe I'm saying this but I see why she's mad.

FUFU

Its not a big deal – trust me Kat

Can I though?
: /

FUFU

ofc! I'll call here
her*
lol autocorrect

Friday 11:55

FUFU

u spoken to Si today?

Friday 16:45

Did you get the insurance sorted?

FUFU

ofc – what kind of question??

Have to check

FUFU

so just got a message from Hester
says she knows about u + JPD

What? There's nothing to know!

FUFU

Pick up ur phone!

FUFU

Do I even know u anymore?

Saturday 12:33

FUFU

Why didn't u tell
me about the letter?

FUFU

Where's the message u
said you sent?

FUFU

I need to know these things!

Do you?

'This is not giving me best friend energy at all,' George said.

Norva sat back on her bed. She nodded. 'It's really cold and short,' she said. 'But I'm not surprised. If Afua was staying behind while Kat was moving to New York, of course they would be tense. Break ups between best friends is a thing, too. People don't talk about that much.'

George nodded. 'I hope me and Norva never "break up" but when we're not getting on, our messages have the same energy as these do. When Norva's on one, she either replies with one word – with full stops – or she doesn't reply at all.'

'Understood,' I said.

'And, Kat is asking about the insurance, again?' said George. 'They're all obsessed by it, truly.'

Norva nodded.

'This bit is wild,' said Norva. 'Afua knew nada about James and Kat until Hester told her?'

'But not only that,' I said. 'Kat actually lied and told her that nothing was going on.'

'Kat's so different,' said George. He shook his head. 'She's not who I thought she was – at all.'

'We all wear masks in public – metaphorically speaking,' I said.

George and Norva looked at me with confused faces. I coughed. 'Ah it's just something Hugo used to say. Perhaps she just wanted to keep her relationship private?'

'But not from her best friend? Nah. I don't believe it. "Do I even know you anymore?" Imagine saying that? Imagine hearing that?' Norva and George looked at each other and shook their heads.

'Taking the situation with James out of the equation for a moment, we know for a fact that Katarzyna has told lies,' I said.

'How so?' said George.

'When we were at her parent's flat today, she told Afua she sent her a message about the note. She didn't.'

'You're right,' said Norva. 'So getting this all straight. Kat sent a threatening letter to herself, with an assist from James.'

I nodded.

'And didn't tell her best friend – and manager – Afua?'

'Yes,' I said.

'This is a whole lot of mess,' said Norva. 'An entire landfill of it.'

54

I looked at my phone, at Afua and Katarzyna's messages and back to my computer.

'This bit about Simon,' I said. 'Afua asks if she's spoken to him today.'

I scrolled through my phone, back to Simon's message. 'Look – twenty minutes after Afua sent that message to Katarzyna, Simon asks Katarzyna about talking to Jessica at Arcadia.'

'It so sick she signed with them,' said George. 'They are incredible. Big leagues.'

'They are?' I said.

'Yup, search up their website,' he said. He jumped off the bed and crouched down next to me at the desk. He pointed at the screen.

'Yeah, that one.'

I clicked the link.

The Arcadia website opened slowly. A video started playing, and music streamed immediately. Too much content for our slow computer to handle at once.

'I hate websites that do that,' said Norva. 'So extra.'

'Look at all that talent, though,' said George. 'And look – there's TrojKat.'

Norva joined us at the screen. A close-up image of Katarzyna's face looked back at us. Her big sunglasses and her berry lips. Her long dark hair framing her face. She looked *exactly* like she did yesterday. Yesterday, before she died.

George stroked the screen. His eyes filled with tears. 'Can't believe it, man. Properly can't believe she's gone.'

I patted his shoulder. 'It will be okay, George. It gets easier in time. I promise.'

'Hope so,' he said. 'This feels terrible.' He wiped his nose with his sleeve. 'Anyhow, let's crack on, while we're here, let's find that Jessica.'

'Great plan,' said Norva. She looked at the screen. 'Click Contact Us. We might find her there.'

I clicked on it in the top navigation. A page opened, revealing tiles upon tiles of smiling executives. Blinding white teeth. Expensive looking clothes.

'There's loads of them.' said George. 'I can see me there one day, can't you?'

'Absolutely,' said Norva. 'Once you've dominated the

charts you can go behind the scenes – look, I've just made you a whole career plan, I should charge you.'

I scrolled through the website. 'There are two Jessicas here,' I said. 'But which one do you think it is?'

'What are their full names and what do they do?' asked George. 'This is my time to shine – what with my in-depth knowledge of the music biz and all.'

I moved the mouse between two profiles.

'OK – Jessica Holbrook and Jessica Wallace. Holbrook is the A&R Director, Wallace is the Controller – I don't know what any of that means,' I said.

'I do,' said George. A&R means Artists and Repertoire –'

'Repawhat?' said Norva.

'– they find and sign the talent to their labels. Controller does the spreadsheets and the numbers. It's gotta be Holbrook. Definitely.'

I looked up at Norva. She shrugged. 'Go with it,'

'I'm right about this,' George said. I believed him. I clicked on her name and a message box appeared.

'What do I say?' I said. 'I have no idea.'

'I do,' said Norva. She cleared her throat and sat up straight. 'Open a new tab and go to mail.'

I did.

'Create an account for me,' said Norva.

'An account for you, Norva? Jessica Holbrook is not going to reply to you, pal. I'm not being harsh − she's definitely a busy woman,' said George.

Norva sat back. 'Burn, but you're right. She is.'

I knew who she would reply to. I created an account.

afuamartey@bmail.com

'Brilliant,' whispered George.

'Great work − now, back to the Arcadia tab,' said Norva.

'One moment,' I said. 'I'm configuring this inbox so it flows directly into mine. This will save me checking the account for a reply.'

'Very cool,' said Norva. 'Ready to write?'

I nodded.

'Ace − add the new email address.'

'Added.'

'Now, subject line, what do you think?'

'Well what we going to ask her for?' I said. 'In the email?'

'Well, we want to know if there was a press release − and if they changed Kat's contract, right?' said George. 'Just ask that?'

'We can't "just ask",' said Norva. 'It will look fake and sound weird; we have to be slicker.'

'Alright − I'm learning here,' protested George.

I drummed my finger against my lip. 'What about TrojKat – request for official statement?' I said. 'That makes sense coming from Afua, doesn't it?'

'Absolutely,' said Norva. 'It sounds totally legit.'

I typed into the big box.

'Dear Miss,' I talked as a typed.

Norva looked over my shoulder. 'No, put an "M" and an "s". It looks better and is more professional. Dear Ms Holbrook.'

'Got it.' I kept typing.

'Afua Martey here. I hope you are well. As you may know by now, there was an accident during the shoot for *Cusp.* Kat has unfortunately passed away. We are shocked and saddened.'

'Wow you sound so professional!' said George. 'Teach me your ways!'

I smiled.

'I am compiling images and messages for a tribute video for Kat's family. And of course her fans. We both know how excited she was to sign with Arcadia. She was very excited to move to New York.'

'It was going to change her life,' said George.

'It already did,' said Norva.

'I know it is a difficult time for all of us, but would you be willing to reply to this email with some words on how you knew Kat, what you liked about her, her contract and the new updates you made to it last week. I know she was looking forwarded to telling her family about the exciting changes.'

'Nice,' said Norva. 'Very cool.'

'Very best wishes, Afua Martey.'

'That's an amazing email,' George said.

UPDATED
MURDER

Time of Death: 31/10 19:56
Cause: Fall from Corner 3
Motive: TBC

EVIDENCE:
Item of interest: Note
Content: Death Threat to TrojKat made from newspaper
letters
Received by: Ben and Diana Clarke
Sent by: Katarzyna Clarke and James Paul Dean
Motive: TBC
Location: 2/113
Delivery window: ~~30/10 23:30 — 31/10 09:00.~~
30/10 11:50

Someone on the roof of Corner 3: 31/10 19:01

To do: Find out when everyone left Bermuda's
~~To do: Locate Sandra (Ben and Diana's neighbour)~~

Suspect	Relationship to Trojkat	Motive
James Paul Dean (JPD - aka Old News)	* Stunt coordinator on shoot * KC's secret boyfriend?	Jealousy? Money? Drama?
~~George Shah (GS)~~	~~* Fan~~ ~~* Working on SB the shoot~~	~~Get Norva onto the shoot?~~

Movements	Questions
* 30/11 18:30 BetterBuy - 5 x newspapers - 3 x Beast Bites * 30/11 19:32 Bermuda's - Tense conversation with HB * 30/11 21:47 Kissing KC outside Bermuda's *31/11 13:45 Romantic incident and conversation with HB in Pap's Office * 31/11 Various times Touched the rope on the shoot	* ~~What is your relationship with HB?~~ Broke up one month ago. * ~~What is your relationship with KC?~~ Engaged. * Why did you send the letter to Kat's parents?
* ~~30/11 19:45~~ ~~Went to bed early to prepare~~ * ~~31/11 13:01~~ ~~Arrives late to shoot for personal reasons~~	* ~~Did Aunt Geeta really come over?~~

Suspect	Relationship to Trojkat	Motive
Afua Martey (AM)	* Best friend * Manager (for now)	Wants to stay in KC's life?
Simon Brook (SB)	* Works on sound * Friends with AM and KC * Used to work in News	Wants to stay in KC's life?

Movements	Questions
* 30/11 19:30 Bermuda's * 31/11 c19:10 In the lift going to Better Buy – seen by NSquared * 31/11 c19:50 Touched the rope on the shoot	~~* What are her plans once KC moves to NYC? Staying in London.~~ * How close are they since KC signed with Arcadia? * Why didn't you include GS in the crew when talking to DCI S?
* 30/11 19:30 Bermuda's 31/11 c19:00 In the bathroom. Away from GS	* How close are they since KC signed with Arcadia? * Can we get the sound files he made during the shoot? * Why did KC need to speak to Arcadia? * What were the changing terms? * What should AM know?

Suspect	Relationship to Trojkat	Motive
Hester Bos (HB)	* Director on the shoot	Was in relationship with JPD? Jealous of KC?
VICTIM Katarzyna Clarke (KC - aka TrojKat)	* Is TrojKat! The star of the show	Attention? Framing someone?

Movements	Questions
* 30/11 19:32 Bermuda's - Tense conversation with JPD *31/11 13:45 Romantic incident and conversation with JPD in Pap's Office * 31/11 c19:50 Touched the rope on the shoot	~~* What is the status of her relationship to JPD?~~ Broke up one month ago
* 30/11 18:50 Heated conversation outside 2/223 * 30/11 21:47 Kissing JPD outside Bermuda's	* Who was she on the phone to? * What was the plan that needs sticking to? ~~* If she created the note, was she working with someone else?~~ JPD * Is she definitely moving to NYC? ~~* What is she going to tell her parents?~~ She was getting engaged.

55

'What's the plan then?' said George. 'It's ten thirty – what do we now? Go to bed?'

'Absolutely not.' said Norva. She stood up. 'You better be on point! We've got a whole list of questions – we need to get out there and get answers to them. Now.'

'I was hoping you would say that, because I am NOT tired,' he said.

Norva looked at me. 'What do you think, Nik? Where should we start?'

I looked over our notes. There was a significant amount of intel. I took a deep breath.

'Looking at all of the information – and, specifically the gaps – I suggest we find Simon sooner rather than later. Let's see if there is anything of interest on those recordings. That might unlock answers to the questions about the insurance, the changes to Katarzyna's contract at Arcadia, and the strained relationship between her and Afua. Thoughts?'

'A most excellent plan, sis,' said Norva.

George nodded. 'Yeah, I'm well into this,' he picked up his jacket.

Yes! Yes!

George's phone.

'It's my mum,' he said. He tapped at his phone. He sighed. 'She wants me to come home. What do I say?'

'Ignore it,' said Norva. 'You didn't see the message, so no need to say anything, therefore nothing to sort. Bish, bash, bosh.'

'Yeah, but my read receipts are on, she'll know I've read it now.'

'Blimey, George – who does that? That's the most basic thing! First rule of spy club is –'

Oooooh Oooooh
Ding! Ding!
Yes! Yes!

Simultaneous messages.

We all reached for our phones.

I peered at my screen.

x**LIVE AT 22:45: TrojKat accident – Statement and Press Conference – Triangle Estate, London.**

'Let's get downstairs,' shouted Norva.

56

George sat still.

He peered at his phone, waiting for the transmission to load.

'Come on, come on,' said George.

'What are you waiting for?' Norva shouted. 'Get up!'

'Does it make any sense to go though, Norva?' George said. 'By the time we get in the lift, it might be over – we'll miss the whole thing. The signal is trash in those lifts.'

'Absolutely not!' shouted Norva. 'You're just scared you'll get clocked by your mum!'

'Yeah, that's partially true,' he said. He hung his head.

'It really is best to see it in person – we'll get to see everyone's reactions in person – it will make excellent evidence,' I said.

'I can't get caught on camera,' he said. 'Don't need the aggro.'

Norva pulled his arm. 'Get up!'

***

The lift opened, and we stepped out into the lobby of Corner One, into the outside world.

'It's absolutely swarming out here,' shouted George.

It was. Behind careful cordons around Corner Three, there was a sea of people, waves of flowers, candles and music.

'Let's get to the HKW,' said Norva. 'The press conference has got to be in there – there's no other proper place.'

She was right. The HKW Centre aka The Hub. That's what it was called before Hugo died. After he was gone, they renamed it after him. It's the place on the estate where any – and every – event is held.

'Yo how are we going to get in?' asked George.

'We're going to have to sneak in,' I said.

'No!'

'Yes,' said Norva. 'We'll crawl. For the second time tonight.'

57

22:44. One minute to spare.

We panted as we wriggled along the floor of the HKW, tired from crawling past the police officers at the entrance.

A long row consisting of three tables had been set up against the east wall.

Three people at each table.

From left to right: DCI Sharp, Pap, Officer Katie Smyth on table one. Ben, Diana and Afua on two. Simon, James and Hester on the third. Journalists with their cameras and their microphones filled the rest of the room. We stood up as sneakily as we could and lurked at the very back, our backs pressed against the wall.

'It's like The Last Supper or something, don't you think?' whispered George. 'Well biblical.'

'A holy mess,' said Norva quietly. 'This is beyond random.'

'What is?' I said.

'This! This whole thing – why are they having a press conference before any investigation has properly taken place? It *must* be because Sharpy still thinks it was an accident – without lifting any kind of finger to try to solve it!'

'We don't know what the Police know,' I said.

'It absolutely cannot be more than us – they don't even have Katarzyna's phone,' she snorted.

'There has to be a good reason,' I said. 'Maybe DCI Sharp has her suspicions – this is a good chance to see how everyone behaves. Anyway, shush, it's starting.'

DCI Sharp coughed.

'Good evening, everyone. Across social media this evening, there have been reports of an incident here at The Triangle Estate, involving singer and songwriter Katarzyna Clarke – better known as TrojKat. In the interest of public knowledge and for a multitude of safety reasons, we have taken an unusual step of making a public statement.'

She paused.

'I can confirm that, tragically –'

As soon as she said "tragically" a murmur rippled through the room.

I looked at the assembled panel.

Pap looked down and squirmed in his seat. Ben and

Diana held hands. Diana began to weep. Afua stared straight into the camera. Hester held onto James' arm while he trembled. Simon drummed his fingers against the table. He looked down.

'– Ms Clarke died earlier this evening in an accident during a stunt.'

James scratched at his face and head.

'JPD looks terrible,' whispered George.

'It's possibly what he deserves,' said Norva. 'If he is a murderer!'

'I'm here with Head of the Tri Estate, Joseph Alexander –,' continued DCI Sharp.

Pap nodded.

'– Ms Clarke's parents Ben and Diana Clarke.' They nodded.

'– and the video's crew, led by Afua Martey, Ms Clarke's manager and best friend.'

Afua smiled to the crowd.

'Any questions for us at this stage?' asked DCI Sharp.

I had a question.

I wanted to ask why she was treating a murder as an accident.

58

May Burton was up with the first question. Of course.

DCI Sharp rolled her eyes slightly.

'May Burton, Cloud News. Alice – I mean DCI Sharp, sorry,' May giggled. 'What can you tell us about the incident?'

James trembled. Hester applied more pressure to his arm.

She leant over to whisper something in his ear and gave his temple a light kiss.

'You see that!' whispered George.

We did.

'We are still working out through our investigation,' said DCI Sharp. 'At this stage, it looks like there was a malfunction with her harness – the carabineer clip securing it may have come loose.'

'Impossible!' James shouted. Hester jerked on his arm.

'Impossible?' said May. 'How would you know?'

James opened his mouth to speak again, but he was interrupted by DCI Sharp.

She narrowed her eyes.

'Ms Burton, you are not here to interrogate the crew. We have – and will continue to – speak to all parties involved as we proceed through our investigation.'

'So why are they here, then?' May said with a snort.

'The crew have a statement prepared they would like to share with the public,' said DCI Sharp. 'Ms Martey, if you're ready?'

Afua smiled at DCI Sharp and nodded. She turned to the waiting journalists. She cleared her throat. She then slumped in her chair and began to speak. Her eyes filled with tears.

'I just – this is from the heart, OK?' she looked around the group, who nodded at her. She took a deep breath.

'Katarzyna Clarke – known to most of you as TrojKat, known to me my whole life as Kat – was my best friend. I shared everything with her...'

'Well that's a lie!' Norva muttered.

'...I loved her, she loved me. She was loved by everyone who met her –'

'And so is that,' I said under my breath.

'– her star was absolutely on the rise,' said Afua, looking around the table. 'But she put her friends, her family –

and London – first. She just signed with Arcadia Records in New York, but before she died, she decided to still be managed by me, and stay here in London. She wanted to be close to everyone and to forge an authentic career.'

Diana squeezed Ben's hand tighter. James threw his head back and stared at the ceiling.

'I, along with my colleagues, Simon, James and Hester,' Afua looked down the line of people and smiled, 'wish to express our deepest condolences, our support and our love to Kat's parents – Ben and Diana, and to you, her fans, at this most terrible time.'

Afua put her arm around Diana, who was now sobbing.

'We want to celebrate Kat's life – we don't want to be sad that she's gone, but to be grateful to have known her. So, tomorrow morning, we'll be having a Service, right here for her. Yes, that's what we're going to do. 09:00 tomorrow.'

Ben and Diana nodded and smiled. Pap's mouth dropped open and he swung his head to look at DCI Sharp, who had her head titled to the side. She nodded.

'That sounds like a… beautiful tribute,' she said through tight lips.

Afua sat up straight. She smiled.

'No further questions tonight,' DCI Sharp said. 'The crew and the family need to rest, and we need to continue our work. Thank you, good night everyone.'

59

DCI Sharp immediately stood up from the table. Officer Katie jumped up to join her.

The journalists began file out and we quickly slipped between them.

'If we crouch between them, we can get out and back upstairs before Pap sees us,' said Norva. 'He'll be coming home soon. One – he can't know we were here and two – we didn't make the Bundles before we came out.'

The Bundles. We stuff our pyjamas with other clothes and objects, and put them in our beds. Synthetic sleeping sisters.

Pap falls for it. Every time.

I pushed open the doors to leave the HKW.

Outside the journalists stared blue-faced at their phones and sucked on cigarettes.

We pulled open the door to the Corner One lobby. George pushed the button to the lift.

Norva leant against the wall next to it.

'Nine am it is. That's the deadline.'

I nodded. 'Seems so.'

'What seems so?'

'We've got until nine tomorrow morning to get to the bottom of this then,' Norva said. 'I don't mind a deadline – in fact I work best under pressure.'

'What – you're going to unmask the culprit at the service?' said George. His hand at his chin.

Norva nodded. 'Exactly,'

'Are you serious?' he said.

'Deadly.'

'That actually would be big you know,' he said. His voice full of awe. 'In front of the whole crowd like that? That will be unforgettable,' he whispered.

'Yeah I know, that's why we're going to do it,' she said.

I looked at my phone. 23:07. 40% battery. 'Norva – I commend your efforts and your commitment to spectacle, but 09:00 is just over nine hours away. We haven't eaten, sleep is out of the question. We don't have the evidence to accuse someone, I –'

'Minor details, nano worries,' Norva said.

The lift door opened on the 22nd floor.

We walked down the corridor to our flat and opened the door. The hallway light was still on.

'Let's move this meeting to the kitchen,' she said. 'You want evidence? We'll get it.'

I put the large container of Exceptional Taste Lightly Spiced Pumpkin Soup into the microwave and set it for three minutes. The microwave emitted a bright light. The container spun around in tight circles.

George and Norva sat at the table. They buttered slices of thick white bread, taking big bites of them as they went.

'That's one of the many things I love about Halloween,' said Norva, adjusting her white wig. Her mouth full. 'Everything is so orange – I love that colour so hard. Reminds me of The Netherlands.'

'Since when?' snorted George.

'What do you know about The Netherlands?' I asked.

'Literally nothing, apart from they're into that colour,' she said. 'I think I'd like the Dutch. Nik – let's go there someday.'

'Sure,' I said. 'I'll add it to the list.'

'Speaking of lists – a quick recap – that press conference,' Norva started. 'You were right about it being useful,' she said. 'It was important to see all that lot at once – in a line.' She bit into a slice of bread.

'Told you,' said George with full cheeks. 'You see Hester kiss James on the head?'

'Very intimate.' Norva agreed.

The microwave dinged and I poured out three bowls of soup. I ate mine in small spoonfuls. George and Norva gulped theirs.

'I don't think the service tomorrow was part of the original plan,' I said. 'Did you see the way DCI Sharp looked at Afua?'

Norva nodded. 'She welcomed it with her words – but not with her eyes,' she said.

I agreed. 'And it looked like news to Pap too.'

'Yep – making that a safe and secure event is going to be a mission – I'm glad I'm not Pap right now.'

'I just –' I said. I swirled my spoon in my soup.

'Go on – spit it out,' said George.

'I just found it interesting how Afua was so good with her words,' I said. 'I would never be that good speaking in public, on the spot.'

'Well, she *is* supposed to be a manager, Nik – that's part of the job. Represent her client, and represent properly,' said George.

'I suppose,' I said. 'Just very odd she hasn't shown that kind of leadership until now.'

I bit into my bread.

A key in the door.

The front door opened and closed slowly.

Footsteps in the hallway.

'That better be Pap, and not Brain Drain Jane,' said Norva. George spat soup across the table.

'What an iconic cuss, can I use that?' He laughed.

'Of course,' Norva said. 'Go for your life.'

Pap appeared in the living room. His hands on his head.

'Girls, George,' he said. 'I'm so sorry I haven't been here – it has been absolutely intense down there. It's just awful.'

He pulled up the empty chair between Norva and I. He sat down. He put his head on the table.

'She was so young,' he said. 'So young! Why did it have to happen? Why here? Again?'

George, Norva and I were quiet.

He lifted his head and wiped his eyes.

'I'm sorry. I'm tired and emotional.'

'So are we Pap – we get it,' said Norva. She rubbed his back and pushed her bowl of soup towards him.

'Here,' she said.

Pap took the spoon and began eating. He laughed bitterly.

'Look at you lot looking after me, when it should be me looking after you!'

'It's OK, Mr A,' said George. 'We all have to look after each other, right? That's what being a community is about.'

Pap gave George a weak smile. 'True, true,' he said. 'But how comes you're here, and not in bed?' He sat up straight in the chair. 'Actually, why aren't you asleep, girls?'

'How could we possibly be sleeping, Pap?' said Norva. 'Do you know us at all?'

Pap laughed. 'Again, true.'

'Once we finish our soup, we're going to walk George home,' said Norva. 'And then we'll come straight back here.'

'Are you?' said George.

I felt Norva kick him under the table.

'Yeah, yeah,' he yawned for effect. 'Yeah, I want to get some sleep so I can be ready for the service,' he said. 'Big morning.'

'No – you're not walking George anywhere,' said Pap. 'You two need bed.'

I looked at Norva, and she stared at Pap. George swung his head between the two of them.

'Okay Pap – you're right,' Norva yawned. 'Yeah, I

am exhausted actually!'

George opened his mouth to speak, but Norva shot him a look which made him immediately close it.

'Tell me about it,' said Pap. 'I have to figure out how this service is going to work. I think I'll have to get some barriers set up – eurgh!' Pap rubbed his eyes. He stood up from the table.

'Ready to go, George?' he said.

'Everything will work out fine in the end,' said Norva. She stared at George. 'It always does.'

60

Laying down was dangerous. Such a dangerous game to play.

I closed my eyes for what felt like a moment. I found myself drifting off.

My shoulders melted into the duvet.

'Don't,' whispered Norva. I opened one eye. She stood over me. 'Don't you dare! Keep them open – you know what will happen if you do.'

She was right. Sleeping was a sentence I couldn't afford to serve.

'Just play the waiting game,' she said. 'I don't know – think about being an actress when you're older.' She chuckled. 'I know that's your life's dream.'

It was my nightmare.

My eyes were suddenly wide open.

'Hehehe,' she said. 'I knew that would do the trick.'

'While you were resting, I got your bundle together – no, don't thank me, no need.'

I looked over at her bed. Two fake bodies lay next to each other. Simulated siblings.

'George is in place – he's ready to go,' she said looking at her phone.

'What time is it?' I asked.

'One thirty,'

'One thirty?' I jumped off the bed. 'We don't have much time at all!'

'I know this – that's why we need to roll,'

I pulled on my jacket and opened our bedroom door. I looked down the hall. Pap was pacing in circles around the living room.

'Yes – I do know what time it is, Colin,' he said in his phone voice. 'The estate is completely open.' His hand massaged his forehead. 'There are numerous routes in and out of The Triangle, so it's going to be quite the job to secure the perimeter.'

I looked back at Norva.

She rolled her eyes.

'I know, he's doing his laps,' she said.

I nodded.

'Then, there is the question of the seven hundred or so residents who live here – who aren't mourners – who need the freedom to leave and return at will,' he said. 'What do you suggest we do?'

We slipped down the hall quietly whilst Pap was occupied on the phone. I shut the front door quietly behind us and we sprinted on our toes down the corridor to the stairwell.

We quickly paced down the steps to floor 21 and along The Avenue – one of three 90m long external walkways that we have on the estate that join the towers together.

George was leaning over the Avenue's railing, looking down at The Tri. I didn't know how he could bear to do it. When he saw us he moved quickly towards us.

'You took your time, NSquared! I was sure I was going to get collared by my mum while I was getting out. The plan, what is it?'

'We need to get over to Corner Three and get into the green room,' I said. 'Without being spotted by DCI Sharp and Officer Katie.'

'We could just walk on over, all casual like,' said George.

'Absolutely not – that will never work,' I said.

Norva reached into her pocket.

She pulled out Katarzyna's phone. She kissed it. 'This is everything we need,' she said.

61

We went down to the ground floor and crossed The Tri, stepping over stray mourners and their flowers, tributes and candles.

I walked slowly. My energy matched by battery. 31%.

Tiredness was creeping up on me.

Eurgh.

I shook my head in attempt to stay away from it.

I looked back at the Halloween decorations in Better Buy.

The cobwebs, pumpkins and lights felt especially childish now. So utterly juvenile, considering everything that had happened today.

I looked up to Corner Two. I found the eleventh floor.

I looked for a light in the third window from the left. Right corner.

Ben and Diana.

I thought about the intense pain they must be feeling. At this exact moment. Unable to sleep. Heaviness in their hearts. Sorrow in their souls.

A dull ache ignited itself in my stomach and a little flame of sadness grew stronger.

I know how they felt. That terrible feeling you get when you lose someone you love.

It wasn't nice. It wasn't comforting.

It made you feel empty. Fragile. Like you could shatter into a million piece if someone gently blew in your direction.

I looked away from their flat. I sighed.

I drew the zip of my jacket over my chin and lips.

George and Norva walked ahead of me.

Their pace was much faster than mine.

They were deep in conversation.

If I put in extra effort – I tried to catch up with them, but I couldn't.

Too tired.

I felt like I was walking through Golden Syrup. Imagine if that was possible? I bet Norva would do it if she could.

I laughed at the thought of her, wading through the treacle.

Yes. I was officially tired. Tiredness yawned in my face.

My mind had gone to that silly place. My legs and my arms felt so heavy.

I wished I was in bed.

No, I didn't. I took that back immediately.

The cordon around the white tent outside Corner Three came into view. Police paraded around its perimeter. I assumed Katarzyna lay under there, doll-like. Just sleeping. Not dead. Death was too cruel, even for someone that mean.

'I'm so sorry this happened to you, Katarzyna,' I said under my breath. 'We'll solve this.'

'Nik,' said Norva. 'Come on,'

She held the door open to Corner Three's lobby.

62

George pushed the button for Corner Three then immediately bit at his nails.

'That's disgusting,' I said. 'After touching those buttons?'

'What?' he replied. 'I'm well nervous. I don't know who we're going to see up there. I don't fancy ending up being chucked off the roof, too.'

The lift arrived on the ground floor.

'We won't go near the roof, I promise,' said Norva.

The lift door opened. Afua's red eyes met mine.

We jumped at the sight of her, which caused Afua to do the same.

'Oh my days!' she said, her hand on her chest. 'Why are you three creeping around? What are you doing here? Don't you have beds? Where are you going?'

George stood closer to Norva.

'Where are you going?' I asked Afua.

'What, are you some kind of parrot?' she asked. 'I'm getting some air and going over to Kat's parents. I'm staying with them tonight.'

'That's nice,' said Norva. 'When we saw them this morning, they said that you practically used to live there.'

'You and Simon,' I added. I looked at Norva. She nodded back. 'It's good of you to be with them tonight.'

Afua smiled.

'I love them like they're my own parents, and yeah it's true – we *did* spend loads of time here. I've been hanging around here since I was five. Simon came later when we went to sixth form. Kat's was always the place to be – her parents made seriously great food, there was always music, and I used to love going up and down in the lift.'

'Yeah, it's pretty cool here,' said George. 'Wouldn't want to be anywhere else.'

'What was wrong with your house then, Afua?' I said.

'Oh my gosh,' said Norva under her breath. 'You can't ask that!'

'What's wrong with asking?' I said 'So, did you go hang out in your house too?'

'No. I didn't have the best life growing up, so I didn't want to go home. We never went to Simon's either. We just loved The Tri.'

'You know what I loved,' said George. He quickly looked between Norva and me. 'Your press conference,' his voice trembled. 'I-I thought your statement was beautiful.'

'Thank you,' said Afua, brightening. 'It was just some off-the-cuff words from my heart.'

She clutched her chest and bowed her head.

'The service is a great idea, too,' said Norva. 'We'll be there at nine, of course.'

'Good! You three want to do a reading, or say some words?'

'Oh, could we?' said Norva. She stared at Afua. 'I'm sure we'll have plenty to say.'

George smiled. 'Lots of words.'

'Are the others speaking at the service, too?' asked Norva. 'And are they all okay?'

Afua shrugged. 'Not really. Simon's gone home, Hester's upstairs and JPD is AWOL. I don't think the Police have been able to speak to him yet.'

'AWOL?' I said.

'Yeah, he went for a walk after the press conference – who knows where he is now.'

'Probably somewhere feeling guilty – I mean isn't he pretty much responsible for his wife-to-be's death?' said Norva, her hand flying to her mouth with fake regret.

'Wow – don't say that!' said a shocked Afua. Her eyes were wide.

'Sorry, sorry,' Norva said. She stared at Afua. 'I spoke out of turn.'

Afua stared back at her.

Silence between the four of us.

'Where did you say you were going?' asked Afua, her eyes narrowed.

'We didn't,' I said.

Norva nudged me in the ribs. 'I left my backpack in your green room earlier,' she said with a smile, pointing to the lift. 'There's some medicine I need in there.' Lies.

'And it takes all three of you to get it?'

'Afua, we're young people, walking around an estate, in the middle of the night, mere hours after we witnessed the death of a superstar. We don't want to be alone right now – I'm sure you can understand that.'

Afua relaxed. 'Yeah, yeah,' she said. 'Sorry. I'm sorry. I didn't even think of how you'd be feeling. If you're up for it, really think about a reading for tomorrow.'

'No, we're definitely going to do it,' said George. 'Actually – I'm going to see if Simon can get hold of some sounds for us. I've got an idea.' He winked at us reached for his phone and typed out a message.

'Yeah, nice idea – I don't think he's too far away. He always used to walk home from here,' said Afua.

'Cool, cool,' replied George, not looking up.

'Right,' said Afua. 'I'm off.' She stepped forward to walk across the lobby. 'I need to be somewhere familiar. Goodnight, OK?'

'Night,' I said.

She reached out to push the doors.

We breathed a sigh of relief and pressed the button.

The lift door opened.

'Ooh – before you go,' said Afua. 'Do you happen to still have Kat's phone?'

Norva's eyes widened and she looked at George and me.

'If you do have it, I would love to give it to Diana and Ben – it would be nice for them.'

'We don't know where it is,' said Norva. 'If we find it, we'll give it to you first.'

63

'Bumping into Afua was well scary – but so cool!' said George. His eyes wide. 'Is that what this feels like all the time? This sleuthing game? I'm living!'

'It's not a game,' I said.

'Yeah it is,' said Norva. 'Constant thrills and spills,' she said sarcastically.

'It was useful, too,' said George. 'We know Afua wants that phone – speaking of which,' he pulled out his phone. 'Nothing from Simon yet.'

'What did you even text him?' said Norva. 'You should have really cleared that with us before you went ahead. We outrank you, so you must obey our rules. It is law.'

'Alright, Norva, calm down. I'll read it to you. He said: "Hope you're doing good, Si. We'd like to do a tribute to Kat, you got any sounds I could scope?"'

'Fine, fine – that's pretty good,' Norva said. 'But next time you ask.'

'Norva,' I said. 'He did good, leave him alone.'

Norva shrugged. 'If he answers, we'll go over there.'

'Yeah, Afua said it was nearby,' said George.

'But she'd never been there?' I said. 'Isn't that odd?'

'Super strange,' said Norva. 'They've been friends for at least five years, nearly half your life, Nik – and they've never stepped foot in his house? A madness. I wonder why he didn't want them to visit?'

'Maybe his mum's a hoarder like on those shows,' said George. 'If that was my life, I wouldn't be letting anyone in either.'

'Could be,' said Norva.

The lift door opened onto the 22nd floor. Norva put her arm across the door to keep us inside.

'Alright,' she whispered. 'Now – there could be a cop out there. Be prepared.'

We stepped out of the lift and poked our heads around the corner.

No one. Zero police presence.

'Well that's lucky,' said George, breathing a sigh of relief.

'Is it?' said Norva. 'I know Sharpy thinks this is an accident – but I would have expected more action, more detecting, and less, you know, press conferencing.'

'Well at least we can breeze right in. Easy money,' said George. He stepped out. 'Time to talk to Hester.'

We walked towards the door. When we reached it, Norva placed her head on it and touched the lock.

'Norva – what are you doing?' George hissed.

'Two things,' she said. 'The first, trying to hear if anything was going on in there, and two, wishing I had The Bunch on me. It would make life so much easier all round.'

'Since you're so committed to sleuthing,' said George, 'you surely should figure out a way to get copies for all the keys. You know, on down time.' He tapped his temple and grinned.

'That would be a good idea – if it didn't come from the person who lost the keys earlier,' said Norva, raising her eyebrows.

She knocked on the door.

I looked at my phone. 01:58. 29%.

Hopefully we wouldn't be here too long. Time was running away.

The door opened slightly. The sound of police radio greeted us before we saw a face.

'Oh no,' whispered George.

The door opened wider.

'What are you three doing here?' said Officer Katie Smyth. 'Why aren't you in bed?'

'Everyone's asking us that tonight!' said George.

'For good reason! Why aren't you? It's two in the morning. Go home. Go to bed. Get out of here.'

'Can't,' said Norva.

'Why not?' she replied.

Norva looked at George and me. I nodded at her, not sure what I was nodding at. George shrugged.

'We saw the press conference, obviously.' Norva said. 'And we thought we could offer some help.'

Katie rolled her eyes. 'Absolutely not, Norva. Go home. Bye. I'll call your dad.' She began to close the door.

'We have TrojKat's phone,' said Norva in the gap. 'I think it would be useful for your investigations.'

The door reopened. 'Of course you do,' said Katie. She outstretched her hand. 'OK, hand it over.'

'Can't,' said Norva.

'Why not?' she replied.

'It not on me, it's somewhere else.'

I looked over at George. His eyes darted between Norva and Katie as if he was watching a ball in a tense tennis match.

'Where is it?'

I knew where Norva was going to say it was.

'It's in my bag. I left it here… earlier?' offered Norva.

Yep.

'Your bag is here?' said Katie. 'Of course it is.'

I thought back to yesterday, when Norva said her backpack would create opportunities. I laughed to myself and shook my head.

'I think I know where it is – can we come in?'

Katie looked at Norva and sighed deeply. 'Fine,' she said. 'But you need to be quick. DCI Sharp cannot know you were here.'

'Of course,' said Norva.

We stepped into the flat. I immediately saw Norva's backpack under the table.

Exactly where she left it 32 hours ago.

I sniffed the air. Spooky Spicy Beef Beast Bites. I gagged. 'It smells a bit in here,' I said.

'You should open a window,' said George. 'Freshen it up.'

'I can't, Hester said she was cold,' said Katie. She stood by the kitchen counter.

Norva's interest was fake piqued. 'Oh, Hester's here?' she said.

'Yes, she's been here since the press conference, working,' said Katie.

'What's she working on? Can we see her?' I said.

'Yeah,' said George. 'Just to make sure she's alright?'

Katie slumped against the fridge. 'I knew I shouldn't have let you in. Give an inch, take an entire lightyear.

And I don't know what she's doing. You can have one minute with her, but you need to give me the phone.'

'Sure thing,' said Norva brightly. She skipped over to the kitchen table, crouched down and grabbed her bag. She pretended to rummage through it. She lifted it, she shook it. She made a production.

Katie rolled her eyes.

I coughed to get her attention for a moment to give Norva a chance to make her handover.

Katie looked at me. I smiled at her. She shook her head, and softly smiled back.

'Oh here it is!' Norva said. She jabbed at the home button as she walked over to the kitchen counter. 'Oh no – the battery is dead. What to do? Now it's just a brick.'

Kate snatched the phone. 'Give it here,' she said. 'I'll let DCI Sharp know I've got it. You have one minute' She pointed the bedroom door closest to the kitchen.

'That's all we'll need.' I said.

64

02:05. 26% I gently knocked on Hester's room door.

No answer.

George prepared himself. 'It will be OK, George,' he whispered. 'It's not a big deal – it's no thing. Just talking to another potential murderer? This is fine, this is fine. I'm cool, I'm cool. It's cool.'

'Be brave, George,' said Norva. 'We'll either rule her out – or you know, die or whatever.'

'Don't, Norv,' said George. His hand trembled.

I knocked on the door again. 10% louder this time.

'Hester, let us in,' I said flatly.

'Crikey,' said Norva. 'You are so cool when you're tired, so fearless. I love it.'

Still no answer.mI banged on the door.

'Look at this display of boldness. I love it. I'm going to keep you deprived of sleep all of the time,'

I stared at Norva. I opened the door while my eyes were locked with hers.

Norva and George gasped and jumped into each other's arms. 'We weren't ready!' George shouted. 'You need to warn us!'

Hester was sat at the end of bed in the dark. Laptop open on her knees. She swung her head around to look at us. Her eyes rimmed red. She stood up and her laptop dropped to the floor. Her face was illuminated by the light of her screen below.

'What do you want?' she said. Tears ran down her face. 'Why are you in here?' she shouted.

We stepped into the room. We stood close to the wall. Norva in the middle of George and me. He grabbed at both our wrists.

'We wanted to see if you we're OK,' said George.

'What do you think?' said Hester. 'This is the most terrible day of my life. I have never felt worse.'

'Don't you think you should get some rest?' said Norva.

'Why don't you take your own advice?' she replied. 'I'm not the one creeping around in the middle of the night! I'm concentrating. I'm working.' She sighed. 'I was so cruel to Kat – I thought if I made James see how awful she was, he'd come back to me. I'm so sorry for how I behaved. I'm going to make it up to her. I'm doing the only thing I can to make this better.'

'Which is what?' I said.

'I'm making the *Cusp* video,' she said flatly. 'Making it exactly how it should have been.'

Norva and George took a sharp intake of breath.

'Wow,' said Norva under her breath.

'Really?' said George. 'That's a bit morbid, no?'

'It's all I have left – making good work.'

Hester picked up her laptop from the floor and sat back on the bed and typed. Her back faced us.

'Are you sure you're only feeling guilty about the way you behaved? This is a lot of tears for someone you hated,' said Norva.

'Yeah!' said George. 'Did you kill Kat because you wanted James Dean back?' said George.

Norva and I sighed. 'George!' said Norva.

'No, it's fine,' said Hester. She laughed. 'I like it. Very direct.'

Hester put the laptop on the bed. She stood up, towering over us. George grabbed at my hands. 'What have I done? What have I done?' he said frantically.

With her right arm, Hester leaned forward and closed the door.

'Let me show you something,' she said. 'Sit on the bed.'

Three pairs of eyes darted frantically at each other.

'Sit!' Hester barked. My heart raced.

We quickly did what we were told. We sat.

George's body trembled next to mine. 'Sorry mum, sorry mum, sorry mum,' he said under his breath.

He gripped Norva's hand.

Hester smiled, sat next to me and picked up her laptop again. I didn't dare look at her. Instead I stared at the screen.

'Ready?' she said.

I gulped. My mouth and throat completely dry. I nodded. 'Yes,' I said hoarsely. I lied.

Hester pressed play on her video.

The sound of *Cusp* filled the room.

Katarzyna's face filled the screen. A vision in white against the dark night. She sung along to the lyrics.

Break the bond
Cut the rope
Let me go
Cusp

On the word 'Cusp' Katarzyna launched herself from the building. I winced and I closed my eyes. I didn't want to see it again. George and Norva flinched beside me.

'No, look!' said Hester. I opened one eye. Katarzyna wasn't dead. She was back on the roof of Corner Three. She was still alive. She continued to sing.

I've got to let you go
I need to be with me
A start is on its rise
Do you see?
The night is inky black
But I'm reaching for the light
I'm never looking back
I'll put up a fight

Hester had edited the footage and completed the video. Katarzyna lived on.

Forever young.

At the end of the song, she smiled directly into the camera.

I don't know how Hester had managed to capture that shot, as I don't think I saw Katarzyna smile once in real life, but it was beautiful.

I looked at Hester and realized that this woman could not have killed Kat.

George and Norva agreed with me. They embraced next to me. George was crying.

'Hester, that's *amazing*!' said George quietly. 'So brilliant.'

'I know,' said Hester. '*This* is what I've been trying to achieve – and now my work is done. I got the shots I needed – I think it looks great. It's a success.' She looked down. 'I just wish she was still alive. It's awful.'

I looked at her screen. 'Can you rewind this, Hester? Go back to the scenes of Katarzyna on the roof?'

'You want to see that bit again?' said George. He shuddered. 'I could barely look at it the first time. Too raw, too fresh.'

Hester looked at me. 'OK,' she said, cautiously. She dragged the cursor on the timeline back through the video. Katarzyna moved and sung in reverse. Katarzyna was suspended in the air. She walked up the side of the building.

'There. Can you stop it there, please?' I said. I peered at the screen. Katarzyna was in the middle of the frame. James' rope attached to her harness. 'Is there any way you can magnify that image?' I asked.

'Enhance, enhance, enhance,' said Norva beside me. George nudged her in the ribs.

'Alright,' said Hester. She zoomed in. The thick black rope was large, centered on the screen.

I stared at it. Where it connected to the small hole in Katarzyna's dress, it was flecked with orange crumbs.

Crumbs I'd seen before.

'Beast Bites,' I said quietly under my breath. I sat up

straight. I looked at Norva and George. They stared back at me. They nodded. 'Let's go,' I said quietly. We stood up to leave. My head spun.

'You're finished?' said Hester. 'Did you like it?'

'Yeah – but I still don't understand why you finished the video,' said Norva. 'Is it supposed to get James back?'

Hester smiled sadly. 'I liked him. A lot. Yes. But I've realized that James and I are over. It's finally time for me to let him go.'

'But you looked like you wanted to be close to him at the press conference,' I said.

Hester's face tightened. 'That was all a show!' she said.

'What do you mean?' I asked.

'We didn't want to be there. It was all Afua's idea. I was trying to calm James down, look after him. Did you see how much he was shaking?'

We nodded. We did.

'James had just lost someone he loved, and then he was paraded in front of a camera. For no reason. Just to announce Afua's service – which none of us knew about!'

I looked at Norva. She was shaking her head.

'I thought it was a group decision – the statement and the service?' said Norva.

'No. It was all news to me.'

There was a knock at the door.

'You've had more than your minute – you need to go home now, or I'm calling Joe,' said Katie from behind the frame.

We stood up quickly.

'Thanks for showing us your work Hester,' I said.

Hester shrugged.

'Do you know where James or Simon are?' I said.

Hester shrugged again.

'James is talking to the police, and Simon's somewhere, who knows.'

Yes! Yes!

George looked at his phone. 'Simon's at home,' he said.

'Good for him,' said Hester. 'I wish I could go home.'

'What's the address?' asked Norva.

'Harper Road,' said George.

'Harper Road?' said Norva. 'Fancy.'

Katie opened the door. 'Out!' she said. 'Go home.'

We turned to look at Hester. 'Thanks for showing us,' I said. 'I appreciate it.'

Hester waved her hand.

'Sure,' she said quietly.

She sat on the bed.

65

'Katie, you've really changed,' said Norva as she put her backpack on her shoulders.

Katie looked at us and rolled her eyes. 'It's gone two in the morning. Go to bed, you have to.'

Norva yawned. For effect. 'Yeah, yeah. You're right, you're right. We just wanted to make sure you had the phone.'

'And see what Hester was working on,' said George.

'I'm sure you did,' said Katie. 'And now you have.'

'So cold,' said Norva.

'It's not cold, Norva,' said Katie. 'I'm not your babysitter anymore, and this isn't a game. I can't be caught between you guys and my old life here at The Tri and my new job – it doesn't work.'

She sounded like Katarzyna.

I looked up at her and I nodded. 'We understand. See you later at the service.'

'You will,' said Katie. She offered a small smile. 'Good night – or good morning, I'll watch you cross The Tri from here. Make sure you're safe.'

'Very kind of you,' said Norva.

***

We stepped quickly across The Tri and, when we were sure Katie couldn't see us, slipped out onto the main road. George held his phone in front of him. Google Maps lit our path.

02:22. 23%.

'Oh my god, oh my god,' said George not looking up. 'It was Afua? The best friend did it?'

'Well, the evidence we currently have is pointing to that conclusion,' I said. 'That certainly looked like Beast Bites crumbs on the rope.'

'And she loves those, big time,' said George.

'She was walking around in black just after we saw someone on the roof,' said Norva. 'She was upset about Katarzyna's move to NYC and being left behind. Real if-I-can't-have-you-no-one-can energy.'

'And she really wanted Kat's phone,' added George. Norva and I nodded at him. 'Promise you'll never kill me when I'm famous, Norva,' he said.

'Well, if you promise to take me to NYC then I won't. Probably,' she said.

George looked at her with narrowed eyes.

'Afua's a strong singer. Without Katarzyna, this could be her moment to shine.' I said.

I thought back to the song, and I realized something.

I stopped suddenly on the street.

'George, Norva. We haven't thought about the song.'

'What, *Cusp*?' said Norva. 'What do you mean? George and I think about it all the time?'

'But have you *really* listened to it? "I've got to let you go, I need to be with me, this star is on its rise, can't you see?"' I said. 'I think *Cusp* is about Katarzyna and Afua. Their friendship.'

'Oh my days!' said Norva. 'I think you've nailed it.'

'That's so deep,' said George quietly. 'Kat's been trying to tell us this whole time.'

'James and Katarzyna must have had their suspicions about her too. Maybe that's why they sent the letter.' I said.

George and Norva nodded at me. 'That makes complete sense, Sis,' said Norva.

'It does, because Hester's fully out.' George said.

Norva nodded. 'I agree. She was caught up in James, but she's not the one.'

I agreed. 'Afua is the strongest suspect now. Let's see what Simon says.'

'Simon says,' laughed George. 'I loved that game,'

'We don't have time for games, George,' said Norva. 'Where's his house? Harper Road is long.'

'The map is saying we're here, but I'm not so sure.'

'Why not?' I said.

'Look at it,' George said. 'It's well fancy.'

I looked up at the tower block. It was half the height of The Corners on The Tri, but infinitely more modern. Glass and chrome. A small steel water fountain poured water around itself behind an iron gate.

'Well, well, well,' said Norva. 'Simon is big leagues by the look of it.'

'He never said he was rich,' said George.

'Do you announce your financial situation to people you've just met?' said Norva.

'Suppose not,' said George. He shone his phone's screen against an intercom panel. There were rows of shiny buttons with small rectangular name tags next to them.

'Did he give you a number?' I asked.

'Yeah, fourteen,' he said.

I looked at the panel. 'Number fourteen. Brook. This is him,' I said.

'Wow,' said George under his breath. He pressed the button.

'Hello?' said the voice. 'That you, George?'

'Yeah, it is – what's up Simon!' said George excitedly.

'Great, I'll let you in – stand back, the gate swings towards you. The front door will be open when you get there. Don't worry about pressing the lift button – I'll do it for you from here.'

'Okay…' said George. The big black heavy gates wobbled and swung silently towards us.

We walked past the illuminated fountain. Norva ran her hand through its stream. The wide glass double doors to the building opened in front of us. We stepped into the marbled lobby.

'What *is* this place?' said Norva. 'This is James Bond level accomodation.'

A silver lift gently dinged and opened before us. The lift was wide, clean, mirrored. Smear-free. Distinctly different to the ones on The Tri. Norva admired herself in the mirror. Her old lady make up had run down her face. She smoothed her black suit. She touched her grey wig.

'I look beautiful,' she whispered. 'I could literally live in this lift for the rest of my life and be happy – I'm not even joking.'

I – and all my reflections – looked at her and shook my head.

The lift doors opened directly into a flat. Simon stood directly in front of them.

'You made it,' he said.

66

I looked around Simon's flat. To call it a flat was technically correct, but in reality very very wrong. Simon's place was palatial.

'This is ridiculous,' said Norva. Her mouth agape. 'You have little steps that go down to your sofa, and that sofa is bigger than our whole flat? It's like a bouncy-castle-ball-pit-hybrid for adults.'

Norva and George roamed the room. 'This is nuts!' said George. 'Absolute goals. When I get older, this is going to be my pad.' He flopped into the sofa. 'Peak cozy.'

'Who are you?' I asked Simon. I stood in the corner, staring at him.

I suddenly realised how little we knew about him.

'Do you want to sit down?' he asked.

'No,' I said.

Simon smiled. 'My dad was a famous song writer.'

'Oh yeah? said George. 'Anything we'd know?'

'Likely, he wrote *The Power Within*,' he said.

'*The Power Within*!' shouted Norva and George in unison.

'Now that's a timeless iconic bop! It's been in loads of ads,' said George.

'And every time there's athletics on, or the Olympics!' said Norva.

'And you can let the games begin, because the power–' Norva made a fist and closed her eyes '–the power's within!'

'Damn, that's life goals!' said George. 'Your dad was brilliant!'

Simon laughed. He looked at Norva. 'Yep, that's the one. It's been very successful. We were able to live off the royalties – and now he's gone, I still can.'

'Sorry to hear about your dad, Simon,' said George. 'That bit's not goals.'

'Yeah, cancer… sucks,' said Simon quietly.

'Do you write songs too, Simon?' I asked.

Simon looked up. 'Yeah I do, a little bit.' He shrugged.

'But if you have all this money, why do you bother working? At Cloud News, and then with Katarzyna?' said Norva. 'If this was me, I would straight up lie down all day, maybe do a bit of charity, act a bit, prance a piece but mostly relax.'

'Ah, well that would be boring,' said Simon. 'I want to

make a name for myself, not just use my dad's.'

'And why don't you tell anyone?' said George. 'You kept this so quiet.'

'I don't like to mention it. I want people to know me for me. It's better to say little and have people guess, then to talk and remove all doubt.'

'Deep,' said Norva.

'Maybe you should take some of his advice,' I said.

Norva stuck her tongue out.

'How long have you lived here, Simon?' I asked.

Simon twisted his mouth and looked at the ceiling. 'Hmm, since I was five? Yeah.'

'So how come you spent so much time at Katarzyna's with Ben and Diana if you have a house like this?' asked George.

Simon shrugged. 'It's beautiful, but it's depressing here without my dad. He died just before I met Afua and Kat. Kat's flat – and The Tri – is so full of life. Interesting. I didn't want them to think I was a sad little rich boy, so I always went over there.'

'So we're privileged to be here, I suppose?'

'You could say that,' said Simon. 'But I know why you wanted to come here.'

He moved closer towards me. I backed against the wall.

'Yes,' he said. 'Your investigation.'

67

I gasped. Norva and George stood straight up from the sofa and ran up the three steps to the landing to be next to me.

'You wanted to know if I picked up any sounds of Kat being murdered, didn't you, George?'

Norva and I spun our heads to look at George.

George put his hands up. 'I swear I didn't say anything like that, I swear I didn't!'

Simon laughed. 'No, don't worry. George didn't say anything to me. I heard it for myself.'

'You heard it yourself?' said Norva.

'Yep,' he looked at George. 'That microphone we used is super powerful, has a long range. It happened to pick up some of your conversations in the green room – and on the roof,' he said. He looked between Norva and me. 'And I know you two have form for investigating – I remember what happened this summer.'

I closed my eyes. This was trouble. Norva shook her head.

'Am I under investigation, too?' said Simon.

'We just have to rule you out,' I said quietly. 'That's how it works.'

I closed my eyes and looked at the floor. This was bad news.

'Well, listen – I have something that you might want to hear.'

I looked up at him. 'You do?'

'Alright, Simon!' said George. I shot him a look. He hung his head.

'Yeah, I heard a couple of interesting things, actually,' he said. 'Let me grab my laptop.' He ran off down his hallway. His socked feet disappeared into his deep, thick beige carpet.

'George!' I hissed. 'You could have warned us about the microphone!'

'I'm sorry – I just go so caught up,' he said. 'I completely forgot. But look – we might get some good stuff here,' he rubbed his hands.

My heart thumped in my chest.

'It's going to be alright,' said Norva. 'We'll listen to the clips and then we'll go, yeah?'

George and I nodded.

Distant padded footsteps got louder.

'Right, I have them,' said Simon. 'Sit down if you like.'

I sighed and walked the steps down into his rounded sofa. I immediately sunk into it.

He might be a murderer – but his sofa was so comfortable.

'Ready?' asked Simon.

We nodded

Katarzyna: What did you think was going to happen?
Afua: I thought that I'd move too. To the city that never sleeps!
Katarzyna: *snorts* I don't think so. Your whole thing is so amateur. Arcadia aren't impressed with you. This was your shot, and you missed the mark. They only want me.
Afua: Kat, you are way harsh sometimes, I –
Katarzyna: Truth hurts.

Norva and I looked at each other. George nodded slowly.

'There's another one, too, from this evening,' said Simon. 'Ready,'

'Yep,' said George. 'Roll it!'

Simon smiled and hit play.

JPD: *crying* I didn't want it to go this far. It's too far! Now she's dead!

Hester: You need to tell them, I'll come with you. Just explain it to them, like you just explained it to me.

JPD: Who's going to believe that I wrote the letter but I didn't hurt her? This looks terrible. I found the key, too. I have it. I tried it in another roof door. It worked. I'm going to up there to sit and think. Get some air, I –

Hester: James –

Simon stopped the audio. George began to speak, but I gave him a look that quickly silenced him.

I stroked my chin. 'Thank you, Simon.'

'So much drama!' said Norva. 'What does it all mean?'

Simon shut his laptop and sat back into his sofa. 'I've been worried about Afua and Kat for a while. They haven't been getting on. They were getting more and more distant, ever since the Arcadia signing back in the summer. Kat wouldn't even tell Afua that she was seeing James. It got that bad.'

'Do you think Afua is jealous of Katarzyna? Was jealous, I mean?' Norva said.

'For sure. Afua is actually the better singer – yet Kat became the famous one,' he said. 'It caused drama.

Afua wanted a piece of that success. Kat consistently complained to Arcadia about the way Afua was managing her.'

I looked at Norva. 'Maybe that's why Katarzyna was changing the terms of her contract with Arcadia?'

Simon sat completely still. 'Yeah. Yes. Kat told me she was thinking about dropping Afua as her manager. I asked her to talk to Afua about it before she did anything – I just hoped they would work it out, even though I know Afua really isn't right for that role. I love Afua, she's like a sister to me. But, she can be jealous and messy. Literally messy. Sloppy. Throwing those disgusting Beast Bites everywhere.'

Norva spun her head to look at me. This was it. The proof we needed.

George yawned.

'Tired?' said Simon.

'Yeah a bit– it's three am – way past our bedtimes,' said George. 'We should bounce.'

'Well, you want a hot chocolate before you go? said Simon. 'I got some amazing stuff from Harrods, you want a bit?'

'Yeah, I'd love some,' said George.

'Ah go on,' said Norva.

I shook my head.

Simon jumped up and ran to his kitchen.

I sat back down on the sofa. My arms flopped down at my sides.

George sat forward and looked at us.

'What do you think? That audio nails it, no?' he whispered.

I put my fingers to my lips and shook my head.

'He could be recording,' I mouthed.

George sat back and nodded his head and tapped his temple. 'You right,' he said. 'But hey! What does it matter? Afua's the murderer, right?'

I stared at him. Norva nodded her head.

'Yes,' she mouthed.

I dug my hands between the seats of the sofa. I felt something crinkle beneath the fingers of my right hand. I wriggled them under the crunchy material came to the surface. I pulled it out and held it in my hand. An empty, scrunched up packet of Beast Bites. Spooky Spicy Beef flavour.

Simon was returning with tiny white cups of hot chocolate. I took a photo of the packet, then scrunched it up and shoved it back into the sofa.

'Thank you, Simon – but we have to go,' I said, standing up quickly. I waved my phone in the air. 'Our dad just found out we've snuck out. He's texted us five times already – we're in big trouble.'

'He has?' said Norva. Her voice rose. 'Oh man, we're in for it. The Bundle era is over.'

'Yes, I just got another message – let's go.' I said. I looked at George. 'Before he tells Nina, too.'

'Aww, man,' said George. He slumped down, staring at the hot chocolate longingly.

My heart was racing. I had to get them out.

They didn't know how much danger we were all in.

68

'I really wanted some of that hot chocolate,' wailed George, when we were outside the flats. 'Did you smell it?'

'We had to go,' I said.

'And face our punishments, I know,' said Norva. She slumped along the pavement.

'No, Pap hasn't sent us any messages,' I said. 'That was a lie.'

Norva paused on the pavement. 'What?'

'I found a pack of empty Beast Bites down the side of Simon's sofa,' I said. 'To my left. That's why we had to go.'

'What?' said George and Norva in unison.

'Why didn't you say anything?' asked George.

'I didn't want Simon to know what I'd seen, did I?' I said. 'I don't trust him, and I am 75% certain he was recording us. I was sweeping for bugs, and I found those. He said those snacks were disgusting, and we know Afua has never been to his house – so why was that packet there?'

'But he gave us access to those files,' said George. 'And they strengthen the case against Afua.'

'What if he gave those to us on purpose, because he knew we'd think it was her? I was so sure when I first heard them but now I'm not 100% certain.'

'But are you ever 100%, Nik?' said Norva.

'I was about Hugo! I feel that email from Arcadia is the key to this. We need it.'

I reached for my phone and checked my emails. 'Nothing from them yet.'

Ding! Ding!
Ooooooh Oooooh

Simultaneous messages to Norva and me. From Pap. My lie had been manifested.

Where the HELL are you?
It's 3 IN THE MORNING.
Why are there fake clothes bodies in your beds?
How long have you been doing this?
You are in so much trouble – you can forget that trip in Spring!

'See what you've done?' said Norva. 'You spoke our punishment into existence and now look? We're busted.'

'Tell him anything,' I said. 'Buy us some time. We have to finish the investigation.'

03:15. 19% battery.

We ran onto The Tri and straight to the lobby of Corner One. We pulled open the door and jabbed at the button for the lift. It creaked open and we stepped in. George reached out to press 21, but Norva slapped his hand away. She pressed the button for the twenty second floor.

'You're not going home, George, not yet.'

'I have to!' he wailed.

'No, we're going straight to the roof – see if James is still up there. Remember, he said he had the key to the roofs. Once we've talked to him, we've spoken to everyone.'

'Oh man, I'm going to get in so much trouble!'

'It's going to be worth it. We'll solve this and you can have some of the credit. Just a little bit,' said Norva.

'5%,' I said.

On the twenty-second floor – our floor – we snuck out of the lift and ran to the stairwell. As we crept past our flat, I could see Pap's shadow in the window, waiting for us. Hands on his hips. I held my breath, but he didn't hear us. At last, we opened the door that leads to the roof and ran up the stairs.

The roof was dark and cold. I could hear the noise of the city below us. The wind blew me sideways, and I felt sick as I remembered the look on Kat's face just before she fell.

'There he is,' said George. He pointed to the corner. James Paul Dean was sitting on the floor. His knees to his chest. Tears rolled down his face.

'Oh god, not you three,' he said as we came into his eye line. He wiped his face.

'We heard someone moving up here, so we came to have a look,' said Norva. 'How did you get up here?'

'That missing key,' he said. His voice hoarse. 'It was under the pumpkin,'

I looked at Norva. 'Are you sure?' I said.

'Yeah. Its flashing was annoying me, so I picked it up to turn it off. It was under there.'

'You didn't use it to come up to the set earlier today?' said George. 'Before the shoot?'

'No!' James wailed. 'I wish I did. I would have caught

the person who was tampering with the harness, and we wouldn't be in this situation and Kat would still be alive.' James sobbed. His head on his knees. 'I would know who touched the harness and I would have stopped this.'

He raised his head and peeked over the side of the building. He looked over towards the lights at Corner Three. He looked back at us.

'I can't believe you lot found me,' he laughed bitterly. 'Three kids. Three kids who have been on my case since I got here.' He stood up. He began to walk towards us.

We stepped back. 'I should have given you more credit – I knew what you were getting at with your conversations over there,' he gestured towards the scene of Kat's death. 'You have no idea how close to the truth you are. You have no idea how this business works, how people are constantly back-stabbing each other.'

'Is this about the letter?' I said. 'The one you and Katarzyna created together?'

James rubbed the back of his neck. 'Yes!' he said. 'But I didn't kill her,' he whispered. He walked closer to us. The three of us inched back towards the door.

'So all that chat about the reviews was bogus?' said Norva. 'Actual lies?'

'Not entirely,' said James. 'Expedition: Intolerable was about to change my life. Now I will be notorious as the man responsible for Kat's death.'

'Why did you do it, though?' asked George. 'Write that letter?'

'To protect her!'

'How?' said Norva incredulously. 'Aren't you all about safety? How is making a threat against her safe?'

'I was protecting her... from Afua.' He sighed. 'She's been jealous and unprofessional, and Kat was worried. We wanted to show her that she was in over her head managing Kat, and the best thing to do would be to step back and let Arcadia take over.'

'So you sent the note to Kat's parents? That's incredibly cruel,' said Norva.

James looked down. 'I know. I know! But it had to feel credible. And it was only to scare Afua, not them! We were going to tell them about our engagement and come clean about the letter after the shoot was done.'

'So that's why you two didn't want the police involved,' I said.

James nodded. 'Exactly.'

'But what about the insurance money you kept asking her about?' asked Norva.

James stood still. 'How do you know about the insurance?

'We know everything,' said Norva. She stroked her white wig. 'You might as well tell us.'

'I was asking because Afua wasn't doing it! And she had to be reminded of the stakes, and the money involved. Kat was no longer her little mate – she was TrojKat for crying out loud. Simon understood this.'

'He did?' I asked. 'How?'

'He's been friends with them for years – I'm new. He's been really supportive and keeping me in the loop with their ups and downs.'

I drummed my lips. I wasn't sure what to think any more.

'I know Kat loved her, but this crime has Afua all over it. I was going to marry Kat, we were moving to New York and leaving her behind, so she, she –' James started sobbing. 'I can't believe she would do this, but it makes sense.'

'It does,' says Norva. 'It really does.'

69

James walked down the steps from the roof to the twenty second floor. He pressed the button for the lift. He shrugged as he got in and wiped at his eyes. The lift doors closed, and he disappeared down the body of our building.

George, Norva and I looked at each other. George sighed.

'Time to face the music,' he whispered.

'I feel like we've been facing it for 45 hours straight,' I said. 'I can't wait for silence.'

'Well, we're not going to get that from Pap,' said Norva. 'Prepare yourself for an earful. And George, if we ask you anything in front of Pap later, just go with it.'

George nodded. 'Same if mum asks you two anything.'

'Nope,' said Norva. 'We'd never lie to Nina.'

George shook his head. 'Rude.'

'So listen. Afua. We're going with her or not?' said Norva.

George nodded. 'The evidence is solid. Everyone is singing the same song here.'

I shook my head. 'I'm not with you guys. Not 100%. I'm not you, Norva, I don't feel things in my waters, but something doesn't feel right here.'

'But if you don't agree it's going to ruin my call out at the service,' Norva wailed. 'This is not the ending I wanted.'

'Norva. This is *not* about you. At all.' I sighed. 'I'm going to keep thinking. I'm going to bed.'

I turned and walked to the door.

03:40. 15% battery.

'Night, or should I say morning, George,' said Norva. 'We'll see you later.'

I put my key into the door, but that was unnecessary. It swung open.

Pap was standing at the end of the hallway, waiting for us.

His face was stern. He was silent.

Norva stepped into the doorway behind me.

'Pap,' she began. 'We –'

'I don't want to hear it,' Pap said low and quietly.

He wasn't shouting.

This was bad. Very bad.

'You've been lying to me,' he said. 'How long have you

been doing that creepy thing with your clothes in your beds?'

We reserved our right to remain silent.

'I'm so disappointed in you two, right now,' Pap said. 'I thought I could trust you girls, but you've been lying to me – when all I've done was try to protect you and keep you safe.'

'I'm sorry Pap, we –' I started.

'I said I don't want to hear it!' he shouted. 'Go to bed, I'll deal with you in–' he looked at his phone and sighed. 'About four hours or so.'

I looked at Norva and she looked down at her feet. I pushed open our bedroom door.

I turned on our light. The duvets on our beds were on the floor, and the clothes we had used to make our bundles were on the floor too. I lifted up a jumper. Ringo was asleep underneath it.

'Wow, he must have been *really* mad,' said Norva, looking around at the chaos. 'Really really mad.' She lifted up a pair of jeans that were on her bed and dropped them on the floor.

'I can't say I'm surprised,' I began to fold my clothes and put them in the wardrobe.

Norva got out of her Aargh-atha Christie suit and put that on the floor too. She rooted around in the jumble of her clothes and found her pyjamas. She put them on and jumped into bed.

'You're not going to tidy this up?' I said.

'Nik, it's almost four in the morning. I need to process.'

'But Norva, we…'

Norva replied to me in snores.

70

I opened my eyes. I blinked three times to clear my vision. I reached for my phone and patted the floor to find it. The area around my bed was tidy. I looked over at Norva's area. It remained a mess. She was sprawled across her bed. Her foot hanging out of the end of her bed.

08:10.

8% battery.

I sat up straight in bed.

'Norva! It's gone eight! We have to get up.'

Nothing.

I jumped out of bed.

'Norva!'

Silence.

'Norva please!' I shook her awake.

'Whhhaaa?' she said.

'Norva, the service, it's happening in fifty minutes.'

Norva sat up in bed. She rubbed her eyes. Yesterday's Halloween make-up stained her face.

'I'm up, I'm up, I'm going into the shower,'

While she ran to the bathroom, I continued down the hallway to the kitchen. 'Pap?' I said. There was no response. 'Pap?'

There was a Post-It on the table.

'I've gone to the service – I don't want to see you there.'

I gulped. He was really mad.

I picked up the note and folded it up. I placed it in the bin. I hated disobeying Pap again, but our attendance at the service was not optional.

I looked in the fridge. No breakfast prepared. Yes, he was incredibly angry. I put two slices of bread in the toaster. While they cooked, I looked at my phone.

Still nothing from Arcadia. I bit my lip.

Norva ran down the corridor in a towel.

'Bathroom's free – let me munch on that toast, and I'll make you some so it's ready for you when you're all fresh.'

'Deal.'

***

After I had showered and dressed, I joined Norva in the kitchen. She sat at the table. She was wearing her old lady suit from yesterday. Fortunately, without the wig.

'Why are you wearing that again?' I asked.

'It's the only black outfit I have, don't judge me – I'm just trying to pay some respects here,' she said.

I couldn't fault her logic. I looked at the table. 'My toast, Norva?' I asked.

'Yeah, about that, sorry,' she said. 'I was texting George. He's nearly ready.'

I rolled my eyes and put the last slice of bread in the toaster.

'I'm just thinking about what I'm going to say,' she said. 'How's this: Afua, awful awful, Afua. Jealousy, lies. Kat's life, demise.'

'Norva, no,' I said. The toast popped. I quickly buttered it and took a bite. I didn't realise I was so hungry. It was basic, but today it was the nicest thing I had ever tasted.

Oooooh Oooooh

'It's George. He's ready. Let's go,' said Norva. I folded the rest of the toast into a triangle and stuffed it into my mouth.

***

We ran down the stairwell to the floor below. George was waiting for us outside of his flat. He was wearing a black suit that was at least three sizes too big for him.

'What the hell are you wearing?' laughed Norva.

'Like you can talk,' he replied. 'Recycling your Halloween costume? Looks like you slept in it.'

'True,' she replied. She smoothed down her suit. 'At least we kind of match.'

We ran to the lift. The doors opened immediately.

'How was your dad last night?' asked George.

'Mad,' said Norva.

'So mad he didn't even shout?' said George.

'Yes,' I replied.

George drew breath between his teeth. 'Wow, you're grounded for life, probably.'

I nodded. 'Probably.'

'I'm surprised he let you even come this morning,'

'Same,' said Norva.

I looked at the floor.

'So, you ready for this?' said George. 'You got a reading put together?'

'Oh indeed,' laughed Norva. 'It's going to go down.'

'It's not,' I said. 'We're not going to do it. We're going to wait for more evidence and only speak up once it presents itself.'

Norva sighed. 'It's Afua. She's the murderer. I don't

know why you're protecting her when all the evidence points to her.'

George nodded. 'It does, Nik.'

The lift doors opened in the lobby.

***

The grounds of The Tri heaved with people. Fans stood behind barriers. They wept. Police kept a careful eye on them – and so did the media. Cameras and journalists and microphones everywhere.

'Wow,' said George. 'I knew she was popular – but this is wild!'

'It's like we're on a red carpet,' said Norva. She waved to the waiting crowds.

No one waved back. Norva looked dejected.

We walked around the corner to the HKW. Two bouncers stood next to Ben, Diana and Afua. They towered over them.

Afua's eyes met mine. My body stiffened immediately. I looked over to George and Norva. Their backs were straight, too.

Afua stepped forward.

'Glad you could make it – are you still up for doing a reading?' She smiled.

'Definitely,' said Norva. She looked Afua up and down and glared at her.

I looked at Ben and Diana. 'We're very sorry about Katarzyna,' I said.

They nodded at me with red-rimmed eyes. They looked exhausted. Like they wanted to be anywhere else. Shell-shocked. Discombobulated. I understood.

'Hi, glad you guys could make it!' said Afua to someone behind us.

I turned around. James Paul Dean, Hester and Simon. James looked like he hadn't slept at all. I suspected that was the truth.

'How are you all bearing up?' said Afua. She reached out to touch James' arm. He recoiled. Afua frowned.

'Ben, Diana,' said Afua. 'This is James.'

The trio looked at each other.

'I'm so sorry,' said James. He burst into sobs. 'I can't do this,' he said. He turned away and left the HKW. A tear rolled down Diana's face as she looked up at Ben.

Afua looked at the floor. 'We're going to start in a minute – go inside, I've saved you some seats – your dad said you guys weren't coming, but I knew you wanted to do a reading.'

'Why would he say that?' said Norva.

I bit my lip.

We stepped into the HKW.

'Wow,' said George. 'This is way fancier than I thought!'

He was right. There was a stage set up against the east wall, where last night the press conference had taken place. Bouquets and wreaths lay like a carpet across it. A microphone stood between them, and pictures of Katarzyna at different stages of her life stood on stands. There was a large picture of Katarzyna and Afua together. Front and centre.

'Afua's really making it about her,' whispered Norva. 'How was she able to get all of this ready in just a few hours?'

'Feels well premeditated,' said George.

'How do you even know what that word means?' said Norva.

'I watch TV, too. I read,' George whispered back.

Pap was sitting in the front row. He saw us and he stood up. His face tight, apart from his nostrils which were flared. There were no seats available next to him. Officer Katie was on his left. Jane on his right. Jane stood up too and she followed his gaze. When she realised he was staring at us, she offered us a slight smile. She pulled on the sleeve of Pap's jacket and he sat down. His eyes followed us to the back of the room. He mouthed something that I thought was *I'll see you after this, girls.*

'He is really mad at you,' said Simon behind us. I jumped.

'Yes. I was telling the truth,' I said. We walked between the aisle of chairs and stood at the back. Simon stood with us.

'Hey,' he said. 'So, when you left, I wrote some words about Kat. I was going to read them out, but I thought it might be better coming from you.' He handed me a folded piece of paper. 'You don't have to, of course – but the words are there if you want them.' He shrugged.

Norva leaned forward. 'That's kind of you, Simon. Really thoughtful.'

I opened up the piece of paper. Lots of words written in thin blue pen. Small upper-case letters.

My heart jumped into my throat.

I'd seen that handwriting before.

71

I reached for my phone.

Afua stepped up to the microphone. She tapped it.

'Hello everyone,' she said. 'It's so good to see you all, but I'm sorry it's under such tragic, tragic circumstances.'

People sniffed in the audience. I stared at my phone.

09:10. 5% battery.

'Please can I ask that we put all phones away and keep this service private.'

I cursed under my breath and put my phone at my side.

'Today is all about Kat – her beauty, her energy, her smile. I want to make sure we celebrate her life, and not mourn her death.'

'Yeah, because you're not mourning, are you?' whispered Norva. 'You're out here celebrating.'

'This is not about me,' said Afua.

Norva raised an eyebrow.

'So, I wanted to bring Ben and Diana up here – I know they want to say a few words.'

I looked over at them. Diana held onto Ben's arm and trembled as she stepped on the stage. She looked at the flowers and the portraits and started crying. They were both clearly overwhelmed.

'We are very grateful to all of you for coming and taking part in this… celebration of our daughter's life,' said Ben. His voice low and monotone. 'We appreciate what you've done, Afua. You are more than a friend to Kat – you are like a sister. You are our family now.'

To the left of the stage, Afua smiled. She put her hand out. Diana took it and stepped off the stage. Ben followed her. They sat back in their seats. Ben stared straight ahead. Diana's chest rose up and down as she sobbed.

Norva leaned over to me and whispered. 'Wheeling out the parents? Despicable.'

I looked back at her and George.

Afua stepped back on the stage.

'Thank you, Ben and Diana. Now – I have a special guest.'

A special guest at a service? Shouldn't the deceased be the only VIP?

I looked at Norva.

She pursed her lips and raised her hands.

'Lunero – Kat's label mate at Arcadia – performed at the GoTo last night. She's here to sing for Kat.'

An excited murmur ran through the crowd.

'Lunero!?' shouted George and Norva in unison. 'Yes!' said Norva.

A very tall, thin, light-skinned black woman. Black jeans tucked into thigh-high boots, cropped leather jacket, large sunglasses walked on the stage.

'This one's for you, Kat,' said Lunero in a strong American accent. A New Yorker.

'How cool is this?' squealed Norva, memories of murderers mislaid.

Lunero opened her mouth to sing. Beautiful tones followed.

Norva and George danced on the spot to the beat and the congregation clapped along.

This service was sombre no longer.

I looked around the room. People smiled along and nodded their heads. I looked at Afua. She was staring at Norva and George intently. She smiled at them.

Lunero finished her song and the crowd clapped.

'This is the best funeral-party ever,' sighed Norva.

Afua stepped back on stage.

'Thank you Lunero – I appreciate you taking so much time from your busy schedule to join us as we celebrate Kat. I wanted to sing something for her, too – something that she wrote. I came across it last night. Then, some young fans are going to speak about Kat's impact on their lives.'

There was a light smattering of applause.
Afua looked at us and nodded.
Norva nodded back.
'We're ready,' she mouthed.
Afua closed her eyes.

I look at you, you don't see me
We're not in the place we used to be

Those lyrics seemed familiar.

No – as you move towards the sun
New life begins, endless fun

Endless fun? Not funeral appropriate. At all.
I definitely knew this song.

No – I retreat, I stay inside
But keep you forever in my mind

I looked down at my phone and scrolled through the images I captured yesterday.

The lyrics were written in thin blue pen. Small upper-case letters.

I'll hold on to your smirks and irks
But you can keep the waterworks.

My heart stopped. I unfurled the piece of paper in my hand.

A match.

Simon's handwriting.

I looked up at Simon. He was staring at Afua. His fist rolled into a ball.

My phone vibrated in my hand. 3% battery.

I forced the piece of paper back into my pocket.

I stared at my screen. An email from Jessica Holbrook at Arcadia.

My mouth was suddenly desert dry. I opened the email.

Dear Afua,

I'm so sorry for our joint loss.

We just want to say how much we were looking forward to working with her, and the world is a much darker place without her.

On your note about changing her contract – no such request was made by Kat and there is no press release incoming! I don't know what's happening on your side of the pond? Someone – Simon? – called and asked about this on Friday? We told him the same thing.

Sending love and light,
JH x

I nudged Norva. I put the phone under her nose. She swayed to the beat as she read it.

When she got to the last line, she stood up straight.

I quickly switched my phone to my images and showed her the lyrics. I pointed to the stage. She nodded. I reached into my pocket and pulled out the note from Simon.

Her hand flew to her mouth. She leaned forward and looked at Simon and leaned back. She touched George on the shoulder and whispered in his ear.

On hearing the news, George stumbled. Norva held him up.

Afua finished her song.

Applause.

'Now, Nik, Norva, George. Are you ready?'

'Yes,' said Norva. Her voice cracked.

72

The three of us walked down the narrow gap between the chairs to reach the stage.

Each step I took felt like it landed on the ground hours later.

I passed the rows of people, and they looked up at us expectantly. They smiled encouragingly. My throat was so dry, while my hands, ironically, dripped water. Or at least, I felt like they did.

As we reached the front, I caught Pap's eye. He stared at us and shook his head angrily. Jane grabbed onto his hand to keep him from standing. Again.

Norva stepped onto the stage. George gulped and followed her. I stood at the edge. I shook as I thought of Kat.

'Get up here,' Norva hissed between her teeth while she smiled. A real skill of hers.

I stepped on the stage and looked out at the crowd.

Hundreds of mourners stared back.

Norva cleared her throat.

'Hi, I'm Norva,' she coughed. 'It's true what they say, the good die young,' she began. 'And Katarzyna was both good and young.'

The crowd nodded.

'My best friend – George—'

George nodded.

'— was lucky enough to meet Katarzyna when she was on tour earlier this year. This is how this whole thing started, really,' she said.

She looked at me. 'This is my sister, Nik. Nik's not that bothered about Katarzyna's music, really.'

The crowd laughed.

'But when she heard TrojKat was going to come to The Tri to make her video, she definitely wanted to be involved. Who wouldn't?'

I looked over at Norva was a quizzical look. This wasn't true. She nodded back at me.

'Katarzyna was stressed out and tired when we met her, but hey, she's a superstar, so we thought it was fine. We were in the presence of greatness after all.'

The crowd nodded in agreement.

'Things got interesting really quickly. We met the whole crew and spent some time with them. They were all so friendly and welcoming.'

George and I looked at each other. What was coming out of Norva's mouth?

'The next day, though, there was drama. Someone sent a threatening note about Katarzyna to her parents, Ben and Diana. They slid it under their door in the middle of the night. We tried to work out who had sent it – and it turned out it was Katarzyna herself who made it, with James Paul Dean, her fiancé.'

The crowd turned around to look at each other in their seats. Officer Katie stood up.

'And we worked out why, too. They were trying to get you to stop being Kat's manager, Afua. They thought you weren't up to the task. Sorry.'

George leaned next to the microphone. 'But I think they made a mistake – because this death party is well good.'

Pap stood up. 'Girls! George! Sit down now,' he said snapped.

'No, Pap – there's more,' said Norva.

'So, we get to the shoot and the crew are all arguing about the stunt. Hester – that's her at the back – really wanted it to look good, but James Paul Dean was worried about the safety. They all left to get dinner and set up, and while we were gone, my sister and I looked over and saw someone on the roof, touching the equipment.

354

We told Afua, and tried to tell JPD, but the crew still went through with the stunt. And here we are, unfortunately.'

'Stop this!' said Pap. Afua stood at the side of the stage. Her mouth hung open.

'To everyone else, this seems like a tragic accident,' said Norva. She looked at Katie. 'But because we spent a lot of time with the crew – we know it is not. It's murder.'

The crowd gasped.

Diana and Ben stared at us. I had to look away. I focused on the flowers in front of me.

Officer Katie stepped forward. 'Stop now.'

Norva spoke quickly. 'At first the obvious suspect was James. He touched Kat's harness, he was in charge of the stunt – but it wasn't him. He really did love Kat, and he couldn't wait to move to New York with her. He created the note to protect her - not as part of a plot to kill her. And because they weren't married yet, he won't get any of the riches now she's dead.'

'Then we considered Hester. She and James used to be together before he left her for Katarzyna. But it wasn't her either. She's realized that she and James are over, and she wasn't interested in hurting Katarzyna – she just wanted to make the perfect video. She's thorough and professional.'

'Well, mostly,' said George.

Norva looked at Afua. 'Then we thought it was you, Afua. We really really did. Up until about one minute ago. The plan was to come up here and call you out.'

'What?' said Afua.

I looked at the back of the room. Simon stood straight and looked ahead. He stared at George.

'Yeah. Katarzyna was about to drop you as her manager, she was moving to New York without you … you had so much motive. But we realized that you didn't do it either. And we worked it out – because someone else couldn't help themselves,' said Norva. 'Nik – you want to take over here?'

I didn't.

'Come on, bring this home,' she said. She pleaded with me.

I stepped forward. I coughed.

'Something was simply not right about Afua being the murderer,' I said. 'The morning before the shoot, we found ourselves trapped in Katarzyna's bedroom. We found some of her notebooks with old lyrics. There were two different sets with different handwriting. The quality of the content differed, too.'

'Massively,' said Norva. 'Like, worlds apart.'

'We saw messages on Kat's phone from Simon asking if

356

she – Katarzyna – had made updates to the contract and was going to send out a new press release –'

I didn't want to say how we had seen them. I didn't need us getting arrested for hiding evidence.

'– and we didn't realise how strange that was until a number of things happened. One: we went to Simon's house –'

'Very fancy house – he's a millionaire,' said George.

'What?' shouted Afua.

'You were at his house last night?' asked Pap furiously. from the front row.

'– and found out he's a songwriter too. Two: there was an empty packet of crisps in his sofa, Spooky Spicy Beef Beast Bites. Simon claimed to hate them. Afua is the only member of the crew who eats them – but they both told us she'd never been to his house. So why were they there?'

I remembered that we had seen dust from those snacks on the black rope of Katarzyna's harness.

I shuddered.

'Three: Simon gave us a note as we came to the service this morning. His handwriting exactly matches the lyrics we found in Katarzyna's bedroom. Four: we reached out to Arcadia – Katarzyna's new record label – to ask about the contract changes. None were requested – but they told us Simon reached out to ask about it on Friday.'

Simon began pacing down the aisle. Directly towards us.

I spoke very quickly.

'Simon said something really interesting last night. He said I want to make a name for myself. He was working with Katarzyna on her lyrics, the handwriting proves it. He wrote the song that Afua just sang to you. He wanted Katarzyna to start crediting him as her song writer. She lied and told him she would – that was the press release she was talking about. We thought at first it was about Afua, but it can't have been. James told us that they were hoping that Afua would step away on her own! But, when Simon got in contact with Arcadia last week and found out that Kat had lied, he was so angry that he tampered with the stunt, framing Afua in the process. It would have been perfect – getting rid of Katarzyna, and getting rid of the other person who was making money from Simon's songs, all at once.'

I gulped down a deep breath. My throat was dry. I had never said that many words so close together.

'You know nothing about it,' Simon snarled.

'It sounds like they know plenty about it,' said DCI Sharp. She stood in the doorway of the HKW. She panted. A team of police officers stood behind her. 'This wasn't an accident at all. Simon Brook, I'm arresting you for the murder of Katarzyna Clarke. You do not have to say anything, but …'

73

'You can't seriously be arresting me because of the word of three kids,' shouted Simon. 'Ridiculous.'

The previously-quiet, dumbfounded crowd had their voices back. They talked to each other loudly. They shouted expletives at Simon. And at us. Some of them raised their phones to record the drama.

Diana shook in her seat. She looked around at the scene and up at Ben. Ben was furious. He lunged toward Simon. Pap and two police officers jumped in front of them.

'I wrote *Cusp*, all of the lyrics – and now that song is huge. Massive. I deserve that credit,' Simon spat. 'When will it be my turn? First my dad, and then Kat. I'm the reason for her success – she owed me, she said she would deal with it, and she didn't.'

'So you killed my daughter, your friend, over a song?' shouted Ben. 'Over one song?' He sobbed. He reached over to him to grab the neck of his shirt. 'You spend years at my house, being part of my family and you do this?'

Simon shrugged. 'It's what I deserve,' he said.

'Get him out of here,' said DCI Sharp. 'Now!'

Simon, flanked by what seemed like an entire police force, left the HKW. An ear-shattering chorus of boos rained down upon him.

Afua stood by the stage. She cried deeply. She struggled for air between sobs. 'Everyone thought I did this? Everyone thought I would kill my best friend? Because I was jealous?' She leaned over and wailed. 'Why would I do that?' Diana put her hand on her shoulder.

'Simon did an exceptional job of turning everyone against you,' I said. 'He was feeding bad information to James Paul Dean about you, and that's what led to the letter. If it makes it any better, I always thought it wasn't you.'

Norva and George looked at the floor. Hester put her hand on Afua's shoulder.

'Don't you touch me!' said Afua. She looked up at Hester. 'You believed this, too?'

'I did, yes,' said Hester. 'You seemed unprofessional. I was wrong. I'm sorry.'

'Well, I don't accept your apology!' She screamed. 'Get out. Everyone get out! The service is over.'

The crowd, eyes wild with excitement at the scene that

just unfolded before them, began to file out.

'I will never ever forget this,' said one.

'This has been the least lazy Sunday morning ever,' said another.

Officer Katie stepped forward. 'I told you to go home!' she said. She tried to keep her face tight and angry, but a proud smile danced around her mouth. Her eyes were bright.

'Of course we didn't,' said Norva. 'We had a case to solve!'

'Yeah we did!' said George.'

'Who's we?' asked Norva.

'Ayy, Norva. I've proved myself, let me in.'

Norva laughed. 'You did good, George.'

'Yes, you were fine,' I said.

'What, that's it? That's my praise?' laughed George. 'So icy.'

Katie's radio crackled into life. She put her hand up. 'Well done. Bye!' she mouthed. She grabbed her radio from her shoulder and stepped out into the bright November morning.

Pap stood at the doorway, ushering the last of the people out. We walked towards him.

'Pap, we're so sorry, we —' Norva began.

'Again? You got involved again?' He looked at George.

'And you roped George into this mess, too?'

'Nah, nah Mr A, I came into this with my eyes wide open, and I'm glad I did. We're thinking about officially making this duo a trio.'

'No,' I said. 'That is not on the cards. At all.'

George smiled at me and Norva. 'Come on, NSquared,' he said. 'Believe. Believe in me!'

SOLVED!!
MURDER

Time of Death: 31/10 19:56
Cause: Fall from Corner 3
Motive: Song writing Credits

EVIDENCE:
Item of interest: Note
Content: Death Threat to TrojKat made from
newspaper letters
Received by: Ben and Diana Clarke
Sent by: Katarzyna Clarke and James Paul Dean
Motive: To persuade Afua to step down at KC's
manager
Location: 2/113
Delivery window: ~~30/10 23:30 - 31/10 09:00.~~
30/10 11:50

Someone on the roof of Corner 3: 31/10 19:01

To do: Find out when everyone left Bermuda's

~~To do: Locate Sandra (Ben and Diana's neighbour)~~

CUSP LYRICS	ABOUT "CUSP" 1 Contributor
[VERSE 1] We're living at the cusp Existing by the brink What happens if we swim? Do I sink? When every day you rise Do you watch me fall? You look back while you run And see me crawl [CHORUS 1] (Don't) Break the bond (Don't) Cut the rope (Don't) Let me go Cusp [VERSE 2] I've got to let you go I need to be with me A star is on its rise Do you see? The night is inky black But I'm reaching for the light I'm never looking back I'll put up a fight [CHORUS 2] (Yes) Break the chains (Yes) Cut the tie (Yes) Let me go Cusp	TrojKat's most popular song – is filled with mixed metaphors and ethereal lyrics, hinting at a demise of an important relationship. TrojKat – a typically enigmatic and private artist – leaves her fans to speculating – and mourning her untimely passing. Read more >> **WHO WAS TROJKAT? 2 Contributors** Born Katarzyna Clarke in London on December 28, 1996, TrojKat was – ironically – on the cusp of stardom when she fell to her death during a stunt for this video on The Triangle Estate, South London. Originally believed to be an accident, Simon Brook, who had known Clarke since she was 16, was charged with her murder and sentenced to life in prison without parole. read more >>

Suspect	Relationship to Trojkat	Motive
James Paul Dean (JPD – aka Old News)	* Stunt coordinator on shoot * KC's secret boyfriend?	Jealousy? Money? Drama?
~~George Shah (GS)~~	~~* Fan~~ ~~* Working with SB on the shoot~~	~~Get Norva onto the shoot?~~

Movements	Questions
* 30/11 18:30 BetterBuy - 5 x newspapers 3 x Beast Bites * 30/11 19:32 Bermuda's - Tense conversation with HB * 30/11 21:47 Kissing KC outside Bermuda's *31/11 13:45 Romantic incident and conversation with HB in Pap's Office * 31/11 Various times Touched the rope on the shoot	~~* What is your relationship with HB?~~ Broke up one month ago. ~~* What is your relationship with KC?~~ Engaged. * Why did you send the letter to Kat's parents?
~~* 30/11 19:45~~ ~~Went to bed early to prepare~~ ~~* 31/11 13:01~~ ~~Arrives late to shoot for personal reasons~~	~~* Did Aunt Geeta really come over?~~

Suspect	Relationship to Trojkat	Motive
Afua Martey (AM)	* Best friend * Manager (for now)	Wants to stay in KC' life?
CULPRIT Simon Brook (SB)	* Works on sound * Friends with AM and KC * Used to work in News	Wants to stay in KC' life?

Movements	Questions
* 30/11 19:30 Bermuda's * 31/11 c19:10 In the lift going to Better Buy – seen by NSquared * 31/11 c19:50 Touched the rope on the shoot	~~* What are her plans~~ ~~once KC moves to~~ ~~NYC?~~ Staying in London. * How close are they since KC signed with Arcadia? * Why didn't you include GS in the crew when talking to DCI S?
* 30/11 19:30 Bermuda's 31/11 c19:00 In the bathroom. Away from GS	* How close are they since KC signed with Arcadia? * Can we get the sound files he made during the shoot? * Why did KC need to speak to Arcadia? * What were the changing terms? * What should AM know?

Suspect	Relationship to Trojkat	Motive
Hester Bos (HB)	* Director on the shoot	Was in relationship with JPD? Jealous of KC?
VICTIM Katarzyna Clarke (KC – aka TrojKat)	* Is TrojKat! The star of the show	Attention? Framing someone?

Movements	Questions
* 30/11 19:32 Bermuda's - Tense conversation with JPD *31/11 13:45 Romantic incident and conversation with JPD in Pap's Office * 31/11 c19:50 Touched the rope on the shoot	* What is the status of her relationship to JPD? Broke up one month ago
* 30/11 18:50 Heated conversation outside 2/223 * 30/11 21:47 Kissing JPD outside Bermuda's	* Who was she on the phone to? * What was the plan that needs sticking to? * If she created the note, was she working with someone else? JPD * Is she definitely moving to NYC? * What is she going to tell her parents? She was getting engaged.

ACKNOWLEDGEMENTS

To the wonderful team at Knights Of **Eishar Brar, Aimée Felone** and **David Stevens** thank you so so much for your constant belief and incredible patience! You are unbelievable, and I am so proud to be part of the Knights Of family.

Marssaié Jordan your design skills are unbeatable and thank you to **Wumi Olaosebikan** for a literally sickening cover.

Robin Stevens remains the best editor anyone could wish for. I am so grateful to you and your mind. Thank you!

Thanks to **Hellie Ogden, Claire Conrad** and **Kate Longman** at **Janklow and Nesbit UK** for taking such good care of me.

Søren Nielson thank you for talking the stunts through with me. I loved working with you and **Daniela Essart** at Scarabeus and I miss you. Same to **Vicki Amedume** and **Camille Bensoussan** at Upswing. Thanks for the inspiration!

To my family. **Daniel Anthony, Joseph Jackson Anthony, Margot Jackson Anthony, Julian Jackson, Leigh Jackson** and **Kristina Kuznetsova, Dean Jackson** and **Samantha Duffy** and **Lynda & Benn Hunter**, I love you all very much, thanks for all the cheerleading and love.

Site Gallery staff are the best.

Last and no means least, thank you to **Fiona Sharp** and **Durham Waterstones children's group** for their incredible support and championing. I will never forget it.

SHARNA JACKSON

Sharna Jackson is an author, of Tate Kids British Art Activity Book, Tate Kids Modern Art Activity Book and the High-Rise Mystery series, and the Artistic Director at Site Gallery, Sheffield's leading international contemporary art space.

She is driven specifically to encourage and increase diverse and disengaged audiences' participation in the arts locally, nationally, and globally.

She was born and raised in Luton and currently lives in Sheffield and Rotterdam.

WUMZUM

Wumzum is an illustrator and muralist from London that works digitally and traditionally. Character designs are the focal point of his work and he often reflects the likeness of people he knows.

Wumzum tells stories through visual moments of music, London's urban culture and community.